Grace Among the Leavings

A Novella

Beverly Fisher

Thorncraft Publishing
Clarksville, Tennessee

First Edition, 2013

Published in the United States by Thorncraft Publishing. No part of this book may be reproduced, by any means, without written permission from the author and/or Thorncraft Publishing. Requests for permission to reproduce material from this work should be sent to Thorncraft Publishing, P.O. Box 31121, Clarksville, TN 37040.

This novel is a work of fiction. Names, characters, incidences, and places are the products of the author's imagination or used fictitiously. Any resemblance to actual individual people, living or dead, places, or events is completely coincidental.

ISBN-13: 978-0-9857947-3-6
ISBN-10: 0985794739

Cover and Illustration Design by Steven M. Walker,
Steven M Walker Images, http://www.stevenMwalkerImages.com/
Cover and author photographs by Shana Thornton.
Front cover, spine, & back cover fonts are IM FELL Great Primer PRO.
The Fell Types are digitally reproduced by Igino Marini:
http://www.iginomarini.com
No part of this book cover may be reproduced, by any means, without written permission from Thorncraft Publishing.

Library of Congress Control Number: 2013938285

Thorncraft Publishing
P.O. Box 31121
Clarksville, TN 37040
http://www.thorncraftpublishing.com
thorncraftpublishing@gmail.com

10 9 8 7 6 5 4 3 2 1

For Kitty Madden

ACKNOWLEDGMENTS

To Kitty Madden, for her suggestion that I write a Civil War novel, her invaluable input and proofreading skills, and for all her incalculable support through the years.

To Shana Thornton for selecting this book for her publishing debut and to her husband, Terry Morris, for all his contributions to Thorncraft Publishing and for being the best lumberjack in the county and to both Shana and Terry for sharing their laughter and their family. To Shana for the cover photographs and the author photo.

To my parents, William and Frances Fisher, for their encouragement and love and who made sure almost every vacation took us to a Civil War battlefield.

To my brother, John Harold Fisher, Sr., who loved all things Civil War and for his comments regarding the book. And, to his wife, MiHyea Fisher, for her tender care of him, our mother, and the rest of the family.

To my grandfather, John Blanton Dorris, who told me the sad tale of his grandfather in the Civil War, and my grandmother, Selma Dorris, both of whom coaxed life from the land for over 85 years.

To Melanie Fisher Cooper and John Harold Fisher, Jr. and Rachel Fisher Henry for their enthusiasm about my writings.

To my brother, Bill Fisher, who, like the "Daddy" of the story, also fathered two girls (Shannon and Sarah) and who, with his wife, Connie, were always an important presence in my life even though separated by many miles.

To my dear aunts and uncles—Joan and Clyde Creasy, Linda and Steve Johns, Barbara and Richard Perkerson, Glenn and Dorothy Dorris, Mary and John Dowdie, Minnie and Don Carter, Jeannette and Billy Antwine, Ollie and Jean Edwards, and Virgil and Martha Edwards—and cousins Clemmie and Mack Bingham, and other relatives who, like the preacher's wife and the grandparents in this novella, nurtured and helped to guide me.

To Adinah Robertson for sharing her stories about her Civil War ancestor and for her interest in my writing.

To Patricia Madden, who taught English at Illinois State University, for proofreading the book and for saying I had found my "authentic Southern voice."

For the early readers of this book, Alex Hurder, Mary Wrasman, and Mary Alaina Madden for all their encouraging words and comments.

To a wonderful circle of friends, old and new, who have listened and kept us laughing, entertained, grounded and rolling and fed for lo, these many years: Debbie and David Boen, Jill Eichhorn, Barry Kitterman, Dan and Mya Rachlin, Wanda McNabb, Joe Huffman, Rita Yerrington, Marge Ericson, Carol Cherich, Marna Maldavs, Lee Gray, Amy Wright, Malcolm Glass, Mitzi Cross, Beth Robinson, Gwendy Joysen, Meredith Cullar, Tracy Jepson, Dede Casteel, Michelle Barron, Yvette Sebelist, Linda Latter, Sandy Strohl, Marilyn Devine, Paula Auerbach, Mabel Arroyo, Priscilla Moore, Steven M. Walker and J.B. Gallegos, Cleo and Donna Hogan, Jelan Nabholtz, Deborah Bowles, Dawn Jones, June Stratton, Stan Bumgarner, Nancy Telford, Ann Madden, Colin Madden, Terri Madden, the Roxy Regional Theatre, John McDonald and Tom Thayer. It takes a village to write a book.

To Zoe Morris for gracing the cover and to her grandmother, Patsy Thornton, for creating her dress.

To Steven M. Walker for the cover design.

To my high school English teachers, Ms. Jones, Ms. Johnston and Ms. Bivins, who encouraged my creative writing and who, like English teachers everywhere, give the gift of literature.

Grace Among the Leavings

1

My little sister is buried up there all alone. For a long time I didn't know why my Mama wasn't with her. No one would say. Bess, they had named her. One-day old, and all she had in the world now was a little tombstone. That's the first thing I got the preacher's wife to teach me. How to read what was on Bess' tiny tombstone:

BESS MEADOWS
Born July 27, 1859
Died July 28, 1859
God's Little Lamb

Someone had planted some daffodils near Bess' grave that get thicker every year. I guess my Mama was the one who planted the daffodils so Bess would have something pretty to keep her company when Mama couldn't be there. So I'd go up there to the grave every chance I got, to be with my little sister and wait for my Daddy to come home from the war.

Finally, he dragged himself home, not much thicker than the scarecrow that Grandma lets me dress up. He was so skinny his own Daddy didn't know him. Grandma did, though. She saw this raggedy thing coming at her, and was so overcome, she dropped her washing. Not to run away, which is what I thought of doing. She ran straight at my Daddy and hugged him, almost knocking him over, not caring that he didn't smell so good and that his clothes were almost rotted.

He didn't look at all like the picture he sent us. That's of a smiling young man in nice-looking clothes. That man had a shiny rifle and he looked like he was ready to take on anything and anyone. And beat them, too. Strong. That's always how I thought of Daddy, even though I don't think I remembered him.

I didn't know who this tired man was that war had brought back to us. His shoulders didn't look as broad, and he sure didn't look like he was 6 foot, 4 inches tall. He didn't seem to have a hope in the world. Even a tiny little one. Grandma swears that he's the man in the picture, and I guess she'd know since she gave birth to him and all. I asked Daddy if he was sure he was the man in the picture.

He just looked grim and said, "I don't know anymore."

Seems like he should know for sure, but I didn't ask him again. It seemed to make him sad. He also got real low when I asked him why we fought the war. He never said. He didn't know.

Some people said it was for slavery. I said, "What's a slave?" They told me that the rich Chambers family used to own some. I said, "You mean those people who won't talk to us in church?" They said, "Yes." I thought why would my Daddy come home looking like a scarecrow so some ol' rich folks could keep slaves and have a pew that you better not sit on? And I couldn't understand how could you own somebody else anyway.

I couldn't figure out why Daddy would fight for something we never even had. And never *would* have no matter how much we stretched the corn meal and wore patched clothes. Why would he sit on the porch day after day, silent with thoughts far away, if we never had any slaves to lose in the first place? Even though I thought about it for many days, I just wasn't content with the slavery answer.

"Grandma, why did Daddy go to war?"

"Forces beyond us. Jesus knows best."

I couldn't figure out what the little baby Jesus had to do with all this killing.

When I learned what happened to Mama I wondered if it wouldn't have made more sense for my Daddy to have stayed home protecting us, instead of being off fighting for slavery or something. I wonder if that's what he's thinking about when he's hoeing and he stops and stares until some unknown sign brings him back to earth. I wonder if he's thinking of Mama or of cannons or of little Bess.

I keep puzzling over the slavery question. You see, some of those Yankee boys that were here were awful mean to the Negroes that came to town. Now, if they had come here to protect them or to free them, why wouldn't they be nice to them? I remember Grandma being real disgusted by what she had seen, and said that those young Yankee soldiers ought to be ashamed. That really puzzled me. If the South had been trying to keep the slaves, why would my Grandma care what the Yankees had done to the Negroes? I really thought it was strange when I heard that someone who owned a lot of slaves could have gotten out of serving in the Confederate Army. That news had made a lot of our brave soldiers quite bitter. So if the South had been fighting to keep slaves, why did the big slave owners get out of fighting just because they didn't feel like getting dirty? Had my Daddy known that he was fighting for slaves? Did anyone ever tell him? Or, didn't they want him to know?

I go to little Bess' grave and think about her. Of course, I don't remember her. I was one year and two-hundred-forty-eight days old at the time she left this world to be with Jesus. Even so, I think about the games we'd play, even while we did the sewing and the churning, the planting and the milking. It'd be nice to have a sister. The worst thing about being the only child in a cabin is that they always know who to blame if something gets broken or if some chore doesn't get done. I wondered if Bess would have auburn hair and blue eyes like my Daddy and I do. Or, would she have my Mama's coal-black hair? Bess and I would have fun, no matter if there was a war or not. We would have done our chores and played our games, and maybe she could have explained to me why it is that even after the war is over, no one seems to feel any better.

I asked Grandpa why we fought the war. It didn't seem to make sense to me since we lost and all. He didn't even look up from brushing the old sway-back mule that everyone said we were lucky to have. He said, "You'll have to ask Abe

Lincoln and Jeff Davis that." How does he think I can ask them? Everyone knows that Lincoln is dead and Jeff Davis is in some prison somewhere.

***

I don't go to a real school. It's too far away and I couldn't be away from my chores that long. But twice a week, after I'm through with my morning chores and all my animals are fed, I get to walk over to see the preacher's wife, and she teaches me and two other children some amazing things. I'm the youngest. The other kids seem real smart to me, but I don't let on.

I asked the other children why they think we fought the war. Betsy Brown, who always has the prettiest dresses and thinks she knows everything in the world said, "So the Africans wouldn't drag us back to Africa." That was something I had never thought of. "Because they started it," was Thomas Albright's view. They thought I was crazy or something just for asking the question. They both decided I was just too little to understand the world.

My Grandma wanted me to learn to read so I could read her the Bible. I don't know why. Whenever I try to read to her she says, "I always thought it said 'so-and-so'." And when I look at it again I see she is right. There are some words that are just too big for me, and she should know that. Still, she wants me to keep going to learn what I can, and I'm glad that she does. I wish I could go to see the preacher's wife every day, but I have too many important things that I've just got to do.

The preacher's wife is real pretty, and she let me borrow a piece of chalk. I found a real nice rock, and I wrote down what little Bess' grave said, and she taught me some letters that way. I'm real proud of that rock, and I keep it in my room. I'm glad the preacher's wife saw how important it was for me to be able to read that tombstone.

The preacher's wife came from Nashville with all its fanciness. I hear that she even had dinner at the home of Mrs. James K. Polk! When the teacher first started to teach me, I'd never been to Nashville, but I'd heard that before the war they had parades and parties and all kinds of pretty things to wear and tasty things to eat. She must really love the preacher to leave all that behind to live out here with all these farmers. But I'm glad she did.

My family is lucky. We have a creek and a river and a nice cabin that's big enough for all of us. Lots of people don't have such blessings. They have to tote the water a long way and live on top of each other. I have my own bed. Of course, if little Bess had lived, I'd probably have to share, but that would be all right.

Sometimes I sit in my Grandma's lap, stroking her silver hair, and ask her why my sister Bess had died so soon, and she said that Little Bess just hadn't been strong enough for this world. "It like to have broken your Mama's heart," is what Grandma said. "It was hard on all of us, of course, but your *mother*. I wasn't sure she was going to live. I don't know what she would have done if she hadn't had you. She'd probably have left us to be with her baby Bess."

I was glad that I could help my Mama out. I don't remember it, though. I'm not sure I have a clear picture of her in my mind, but Grandma tells me about her sometimes when I ask.

"I remember the first day I ever saw her. Her folks moved here when she was about fourteen. She came into the church and your Daddy perked right up, and it wasn't three months before he was telling us he wanted to marry her. We tried to talk him out of it. He was just barely sixteen himself. He was a hard worker, though, and I thought that just maybe he could support a wife. I told him, 'First, you build a room onto this cabin for her.' Your Grandpa said he'd mark off some land for him, and if he earned some money on his tobacco, he could marry." As she told me this, my Grandma stared out at the field. My Daddy was trudging across it real slowly. "In three months he had the room built and his own money. All that on top of all the other chores." I looked at my Daddy, too. How could that slow-moving man have done all that? Where was that man who had made a home for a bride so quickly? He couldn't be the same man who could barely make it to the field and back.

"So we had to say yes, he could marry. Course, he had to convince her." She laughed. "That didn't seem to take too much doing," she said proudly.

So my Mama had come to live here on the farm. And I came to join them after that. Then, little Bess. I never tired of hearing how I came to be. I never stopped feeling the loss of little Bess.

2

My earliest memory is of my Grandma crying. Some news from someone coming up the road was always a source of excitement or sadness. It was hardly ever a thing you'd call lukewarm.

This time my Grandma had cried, the preacher had come and brought us news of the war. He'd read a paper, or someone would come tell him something that they'd heard which may or may not have been the gospel truth, but he'd make his rounds delivering the news anyway. I think the preacher would have made a living bringing the bad news of this world instead of the good news of the next if he'd had enough people around him who could read. As it was, though, he always had to deliver his news in person. He'd bring his map with him and show where this or that had happened. We'd all stop whatever we were doing to hear what the preacher had to say.

So my first memory is of my Grandma crying over some news that the preacher had brought. At first I wasn't sure whether they were tears of joy or of sorrow, but I thought I'd better cry, too. Now that I'm older I've decided that my Grandma's tears were for both. Tears of joy that her son wouldn't have bullets coming at him anymore. Tears of sorrow that her son was now in a stinking prisoner-of-war camp, and she'd see him again only if he didn't starve to death or die of some disease that comes from putting too many men in too small a pig pen.

I figured out later that she got this news about two months after we lost my Mama. So, I think she was also crying over lost love. I'm old enough now to know that real love is a rare thing, a beauty for everyone around. When it's gone, well, I guess it's only natural that that passing deserves a few tears.

The preacher also told us that day that the Gentrys, our neighbors over the ridge, had lost their only son. When Grandma heard that news, she went silently to the kitchen and started to cook something to take to comfort the family. She didn't say anything until she was finished and said, "Grace, let's go." I walked with her down the road until she reached the narrow path that would lead us to the Gentrys. She paused when she got there and breathed in all of nature. I watched her closely and it made her seem less weary and a little younger, as if at this little spot she found a sweet breath of peace. I looked down and saw a toad and had to get down on all fours and hop just like it. She looked down at me and smiled widely, and I could feel that for a moment she forgot all her troubles of this world. From time to time she called me her jolt of joy, and I guess right then she was getting one of them jolts.

We walked some more, higher and higher, past the dogwoods and the redbuds—the heralds of spring—as my Grandma called them. The woods had come alive after a long time sleeping, and it was sad to think that even this would not be enough to cheer my Grandma for long. We reached our neighbor's clearing and I was fixin' to run ahead, but Grandma stopped me. She said, "Grace, this family has suffered a grievous loss. They need more tenderness than this world can ever give them."

"Yes, ma'am."

We walked a little bit farther and we were almost to the house when I asked, "Grandma, why is there so much loss?" For by now I had seen little birds die, puppies killed by foxes, and mama dogs too tired to get up again.

Grandma looked up at the sky as if she was looking for the answer there. She said, "Honey, I don't know. To make room for more life, I suppose."

"Is that why the Gentrys have lost their son?" I asked.

Grandma thought for a moment. "I can't think of any good reason for that. War leaves its scar on every generation. The best we can do is to try to stay out of its way."

We walked almost up to the house and I asked, "Grandma, didn't Tom Gentry fight for the Yankees?"

"Yes, Grace."

"Then, why are we here?"

She looked at me with some disappointment; then her face changed and she knelt down and took my face in her hands. "Because grief knows no borders."

I stopped asking questions. We went into the sad house and gave what comfort we could. They had so much food already, and I ate and ate and watched the workings of sorrow until I fell asleep. Grandma woke me, saying it was time to go. My Grandpa had come while I had been sleeping and we walked home in the silence of the moonlight. I walked between them holding their hands and we never lost our way even for a minute. If I live to be a hundred, I don't think I'll know a sadder night.

***

Grandpa left Ireland before the potato famine struck. Still, he said life was plenty hard there. So, he decided to save what little money he had earned to come to America. He met Grandma in Pennsylvania as he was making his way south. I guess that means that she was a Yankee for awhile. Maybe that's why she doesn't say much bad about them.

Grandma told Grandpa that she'd marry him if he'd abandon his Catholic ways. That's why I'm a Baptist. I don't think he did, though. Oh, I'm not saying he worships Mary's statue or anything like that, but I've seen him out in the woods making these strange signs across his chest. I've learned to do them, too, but I don't show anybody.

15

Grandma says they left Pennsylvania as man and wife, and started walking. They'd work for awhile in fields or in houses, save what they could, and walk some more. They'd lost babies along the way. Maybe that's why they kept going, to try to leave the sorrows behind. Finally, when they'd given up hope of having a family, a baby lived. That was my Daddy. They kept walking and working, and ended up here in Tennessee when my Daddy was three. They took one look at the plentiful water and tall tulip poplars and said, "This is it." These hills, well, who wouldn't want to live here?

They didn't have enough to buy the farm outright, so they made a bargain with the man who owned it—some money down and one-third of the crop for ten years. They even signed a piece of paper, although they wouldn't have known what it said, because they can't read like I can. After working the land for six years, they asked the old preacher to read that piece of paper. When they learned that it said fifteen years instead of ten, well, you can just imagine how mad my Grandpa and Grandma were. The preacher, too. They went over to see that bad man who suddenly recollected that the agreement had really been ten years. Of course, this was after my Grandpa convinced him ten years would be better for his health, and the preacher convinced him he was going to hell. That hell sure comes in handy at times.

That's how the farm came to us—through hard work, sacrifice and firmness in the face of injustice. That's what my Grandma and Grandpa have taught me. I'd like to be able to say what my Mama and Daddy have taught me, but those memories are dim to me, if I remember them at all. The stories I pull from my Grandma help me form a picture, but still I don't think it compares to actually having your own parents say, "Do this, don't do that. Kiss me and run to bed. You better eat that or I'm going to wear you out." I look at other children when they are with their parents—even when the parents are yelling or spanking—and I think that those children don't know what treasure is. I guess you have to be without your treasure to know how valuable it was.

Still, I guess you could say that I have it luckier than most. There's only three of us to feed. Plus the animals. Of course, there's only three of us to work, and though my Grandma and Grandpa don't complain, I know that their bones ache, and they could use some help and a little bit of rest. But there's no one to hire, and no way to pay them. I try my best to grow up fast, but even hanging from the trees doesn't make me much taller. So I try to do my best with the body I have, and try not to whine too much. At least to no one but little Bess who, I think, understands.

3

We have to work so hard during the week, but on Sundays we get to stop and go to church. I sure like that day of rest. It seemed like such a good idea that I tried to talk Grandma into letting us have more than one day of rest. I reasoned that if one was good, why not two? She just smiled and said, "No, dear," in that way that means that she's not going to give in. So I didn't bring it up again. At least, not more than once or twice.

So we have to settle for just that one day. Of course, we have to work harder on Saturday to get ready for Sunday. Grandma cooks extra so she can take the day off, too. I have to take a bath on Saturday night in the washtub, and I have to make several trips to the creek to fill it up.

On Sunday, we wake up with the sun as usual and start to get ready because the church is not all that near to us. I carefully look over my best dress to be sure that it's as clean as can be. Still, Grandma checks it to be sure. My Grandpa gets his curly salt-and-pepper hair all slicked back, and he even brushes the sway-back mule to make him look better. He always says, "We don't have much, but we take pride in what we've got."

I say, "Yes sir," and help him get the mule as shiny as he can be. The mule seems to like getting fancied up once a week.

If we have a wagon, we all climb in and head off to church. Sometimes we don't have one, though. The Yankees took one, and Grandpa had to build another. He had to trade that one for some food, and again he had to build another. Even the Confederates took one, and he was building again. I'm tired of everyone helping themselves to what we have. I know that Grandma likes it better when we can arrive sitting pretty in the wagon instead of sinking into the sway-back mule. I've never heard Grandpa say he loved Grandma, but I know that he does, because Grandpa always does whatever he can to be sure that she's got a wagon.

Sometimes even before church gets started, there'll be people off outside of the church singing. I have to say that except for playing outside with the other children, singing is my favorite thing about church. Of course, not everyone can sing, and there are some members that can't remember the words. Old Man Hanson just says whatever comes into his head. Sometimes he even puts the words of one hymn with the tune of another. Some of the boys laugh about that, but I can't, because my Grandma looked real disappointed with me when I did once. On the way home, my Grandma said, "The Bible says to make a joyful noise unto the Lord. It doesn't say it has to sound good." I could understand her point, and I tried not to be too pained by Old Man Hanson's singing. I think we could help Mr. Hanson's problem by having hymn books or even a piano, but Grandma said she didn't see that happening until after the war. Of course, we used to have a piano, but some Yankees hauled it off for a dance hall. Grandma almost cries when she thinks about that piano and where it is and how hard they worked to get it in the first place. The preacher has a hymn book, and if it's a hymn we don't know well, he'll sing the first line and we'll sing it right after him. Of course, we know most of the hymns, so the preacher doesn't have to sing the first line that often.

There comes the time in every service when the preacher has to get up and yell. I don't know why he has to get so worked up on Sunday mornings, because he seems real calm the rest of the time. He's got to yell about needing money, and loving thy neighbor, even if he is a good-for-nothing Yankee lover, and how Christ our Lord died for my sins when I'm not even sure what I've done wrong. I try to listen, because Grandma says that it is real important to, but I have to say that I do get a lot of napping done during that time. I wonder if a lot of other people aren't napping too, because on Monday, I see people who just go back to their same old ways. I know that Mr. Bennett is off making moonshine, and Chris and Henry Shaeffer are off gambling with the Yankees, and Mr. Ross is coveting his neighbor's wife, because I've seen them kissing in the moonlight. I've tried to stay awake during the sermon to see if they've been sleeping in church, too, but I haven't caught them yet.

The preacher also says it's wrong to lie. Oh, he says it a different way. "Thou shalt nots"—that's what he's fond of saying. I wish he'd let us know what we *can* do. I wonder if he means it when he says we can't lie, because I have heard him lie to a Yankee who came to his house looking for food to steal. I heard him say, "No, we don't have any chickens" when I knew good and well that they did. I wonder if there are some exceptions he's not yelling about on Sundays. When I asked my Grandpa about it he said, "It's hard to be honorable in dishonorable times." I also wonder why the preacher skips over the "Thou shalt not kill," these days. Wouldn't a sermon on that bring this war to an end?

I've often wondered why God doesn't send Elijah down in his chariot to put a stop to this war. I've heard the strangest thing. The Yankees think God is on their side! How could that be? Everyone knows that God is on ours. I wonder if it's possible that God sits out every war, too ashamed about what he sees his children doing in his name.

If we're lucky, somebody will invite us over for Sunday dinner. If that happens, we bring the best we have to offer that week, and they spread out their best, and we have more to choose from. I like it when the families have kids that are about my age. Otherwise, I have to sit in the kitchen with the women bouncing the babies, or on the porch with the men discussing the war. If there are children, though, we go for walks and look at all the animals on the farm. Most of the animals like to be petted and scratched behind the ears. I think most of the animals enjoy my repeating what I remember of that morning's sermon and find earthly comfort from hearing the hymns we sang that day.

After we've eaten and said all there is to say, we start the journey back to our farm. Sometimes we don't get back until almost dark, and Grandpa has to rush to check on all the animals. Even though we aren't supposed to do any work on Sunday, he thinks it's fine to stretch the Good Book far enough to be sure that all the animals are not caught in fences or fallen down a hole, and have enough food and water. Even Grandma doesn't say a word against that.

I have to change out of my best clothes. Grandma and I will get together a small meal and talk about all the work we need to do tomorrow. When Grandpa comes back in, we say a prayer and eat in silence until Grandma says it's time to count our blessings. She makes sure to do this every Sunday. I always list Grandma and Grandpa and all my animals and Little Bess' grave. Grandma says that I'm her blessing. Grandpa agrees, and adds that they are blessed that week because we haven't heard that Daddy is dead. The silence returns after that until I take the Bible from the mantel and read until my Grandma tells me it is time to go to bed. I say my prayers, and we say our goodnights and we go to bed to gain strength for the work we have to do that week.

4

There's a tree near little Bess' grave that I like to go visit when I'm not doing my chores. It's a giant shagbark hickory that couldn't take the high winds one day. It looks like an elegant gentleman taking a very formal bow to welcome you. I usually curtsey to greet it. At dusk, I sit there listening to the tree frogs singing and the crickets reply, and think about how pleasant life would be if there was no war, and Bess, my Mama and Daddy were here for a picnic.

Sometimes I like to go up there and think about Mr. Shakespeare. He was some man in old England who liked to use a lot of words to say something simple. The preacher's wife loves his complete works, and pulls them out to read to us about as often as she pulls out the Bible. She says it's a good way to learn history and English, but nobody I know talks like that. I tried to speak that way one night. When

Grandma said to take something out to the barn, I said, "Dear Lady, I beseech thee to not require me to transport myself at this late hour, hence I should needs be already weary from the long day's work."

She said, "What?" and I could tell that she was getting mad, and so I said, "Yes, ma'am" real quick and went straight to the barn like she said. You didn't dare dawdle around Grandma. She'd be the first to say, "Git in here right now," in such a way that you knew you'd better get your little legs moving, no matter how tired you were. Otherwise, it was guaranteed that you'd be snatched bald-headed.

Anyway, Mr. Shakespeare seems to like to talk a lot in a fancy way about who's the king, and who's raising this army, and who has the most power, and who should win this war. After listening to all of that and thinking on this war that we're in, I came to conclude that war was just an excuse for men to get together and avoid chores.

One day, at the broken tree, I saw a bear come by with two of her cubs. My Grandpa always told me to be real still if I came upon any wild animal, particularly one with babies, so I was. I just watched that beautiful sight until it was safe for me to get up and run home. I was thinking that we'd have some tasty bear stew that night. But then I got to wondering what would happen to the little bear cubs if Grandpa killed the Mama. I was old enough then to know what would happen. Grandpa would have to kill them, too, or just let them starve. I didn't like the thought of either one of those choices. So, I decided not to say a word, even though that night our supper was sparse. I didn't regret it one bit, though, and it gave me pleasure day after day to think that that family of bears is still living in those hills, taking pleasure in just being together and walking in the mornings, and rolling in the dew, minding their own business just like God wanted.

***

The mourning doves around here live up to their names. They choose to perch in the trees near Bess' grave, and call to one another. They walk around her grave as if they are the caretakers. Grandma says that they mate for life. I wonder what happens when one of them dies. Do they keep singing their sad song when there is no one left to answer?

While I'm up here, I sometimes try to think of new places we could hide things from the Yankees. You've got to be good at hiding to survive this war. At first, Grandpa and Grandma wouldn't tell me much, because they said I'd blurt it out to the first Yankee I saw. Just because I did it once, they have a hard time believing I wouldn't do it again. They said that they had just told the Yankee they had no eggs, and he was about to leave when he turned to me and said, "Little girl, where are the eggs?" And I proudly showed him I knew where they were. I felt real bad about that, because not only did we lose the eggs, but they shoved Grandpa around a bit. After that, Grandpa or Grandma would march off with whatever they were hiding, and wouldn't let me watch. Finally, when I was bigger and realized the importance of it, they showed they trusted me by letting me know where things were, and I proved their trust was well placed. The next time a Yankee asked me where something was, I'd say, "Sir, we haven't had that since I was a baby." I'd be so convincing that no one ever asked me more questions about it. I didn't tell them that the cow was two hills over in a holler, or that the goat was fenced in next to the creek or that the pigs were sleeping soundly in a cave. Those secrets will die with me.

Of course, we could have helped out the Yankees, and they would have given us orders of protection. We could have agreed to sell them our eggs and chickens and corn, but now, Grandma wouldn't hear of that. She said she'd do nothing to hurt the Yankees, but she sure wasn't going to sell to them. Unless a soldier was sick or injured, she didn't want to make their time here any easier. The easier it was for them to stay, she thought, the longer it would take my Daddy to come home.

Plenty of our neighbors did do things to hurt the Yankees. A Yankee soldier knew better than to walk alone anywhere, because he'd turn up dead. Lots of their stuff got stolen, but I guess that was not wrong, because they probably had stolen it from somebody else. I even heard that two ladies placed barriers on the railroad tracks. The Yankee general in Gallatin, who I hear is real mean, well, everybody thought he was going to hang them. After he scared them and their families, he let them go with a stern talking-to, and told them not to do anything against the Yankees again.

We did not rejoice when we heard of a Yankee getting killed, because it meant that soon the Yankee general would be issuing orders to kill someone in the county. It didn't seem to matter to him who it was, just that someone had to pay. It meant that men would be dragged from their houses and shot in front of their families, or hanged in a nearby tree while the house was torched. Grandma was always nervous when Grandpa left the farm, for fear that he'd be the one taken that day to pay for the life of a young Yankee soldier. So he'd stick close to us, and if he had to leave, he tried to walk along the little-known paths, hardly big enough for a skinny dog to use, to get to where he was going.

I could tell that Grandma and Grandpa were real scared of losing the farm. They couldn't hang on to it if they couldn't keep us fed; otherwise, why stay on the farm? Of course, taxes had to be paid to whatever government was in power, be they the Yankees or be they the Confederates. That didn't stop just because there was a war. On top of all that, the Yankee general could decide that my folks didn't own the farm anymore. He kept demanding that the citizens take the oath of allegiance to the union. Grandma and Grandpa said they wouldn't have any problem with that, considering they had been part of the union for so long before all the mess started. The problem they had was that Daddy had given up his freedom for the South. They said they couldn't do it because they thought it would hurt Daddy. They tried to lay low, and no one came to bother them and we thought we were out of danger. Then some Yankees knocked Grandpa off the sway-back mule and took that poor creature. That sure riled my Grandma.

Grandpa said to forget about it, but Grandma asked how could they do that? They had to get in a crop, and two old people and one little girl couldn't do it by themselves. She went charging down the road to Gallatin. She said she marched up to that Yankee general, right past his sentries and his staff, I mean, *everybody*. She said we needed that sway-back mule back right now! She said that he ought to be ashamed of himself, stealing from poor folks. She said that our family had never done him any harm, that that scrawny mule would not be any good to the Union army or as anything to eat—that it *would* mean something to us and could mean the difference between living and starving. His sentries stared at her in amazement, then were about to drag her out and maybe even shoot her for disrespecting the general, but the general said, "No, leave her alone." Then he turned to my Grandma and said, "Ma'am, if the southern soldier is as brave and foolhardy as you, this war will never end." He asked Grandma her name and where she lived, and she told him. He asked if she had any sons in the war, and she said she had to say yes. The general said, "You know I can take your farm and put you off the land just for that. I can declare that your farm is vacant."

Grandma said he looked kinda mean when he said it, and she said she could feel her knees start to buckle. She thought she had done it then—lost the land just because she was fighting over that silly mule.

Grandma did some fast talking then. She said, "How can you do that to a nice Pennsylvania girl?" The general had some relatives from there and spoke of it fondly. She said they both talked as civilly as if they had met at some dinner on the grounds, just like there wasn't a war at all.

Then the general asked about Daddy. "Where is he serving?"

"I don't know whether you can say he's serving at all. He's a prisoner of war at Camp Douglas, Illinois."

The general looked grave. "That's a terrible place. It was meant for 3,000 prisoners and it's overflowing." After he said that, Grandma said he looked like he regretted saying it. I guess she must have looked devastated. He grabbed a pen and a piece of paper, wrote out something and called for a sentry. He looked back at Grandma. "Do you promise not to use your farm to harm my soldiers in any way?"

"Yes sir, I can promise that. All I want to do is hang onto the farm long enough for my son to come home. That's the only war I'm fighting."

The general gave the piece of paper to the sentry. "Give this lady her choice of horses or mules."

Grandma said she was a little surprised at the offer he had made and said, "No sir. All I want is what is mine."

It was the general's turn to look surprised. "We've got some fine stock out there." He saw the determined look on Grandma's face and laughed. "I guess there's no use arguing." To the soldier, he ordered, "Find her mule." He got up from his desk, shook her hand and walked her to the door. The last thing he said to her was, "Ma'am, you make me wonder why we are fighting this war."

So we kept our farm and our mule. Grandma kept her promise. She never did any harm to the Yankees. Course, I don't think she would have harmed them anyway, no matter what she said to the general. She took no part in tormenting the Yankees, and wouldn't let my Grandpa do anything mean either, although sometimes his Irish spirit rose up and he wanted to fight them. She didn't have to argue too much, though, because we had been witness to a terrible event. We had been walking along the railroad tracks to go trade some goods with a neighbor when we heard the train approaching. We got off the tracks to see the powerful locomotive thunder by with its load of Yankee soldiers and some pretty ladies at the windows. It wasn't five minutes later that we heard a crash and knew that the train had flown off the tracks. We ran ahead to watch from a hill as the Confederate guerrillas massacred the soldiers that were still alive, and stole the supplies before they put torches to the train. After they left in a hurry, Grandma told me to wait while she and Grandpa went to see if there were survivors. They walked among the dead until Grandma quickly knelt down and wrapped her shawl around something. She and Grandpa rushed back to me and showed me a whimpering baby. Grandma said she'd been lying next to a young woman and child. They were both dead.

We headed home as fast as we could with a baby that could be injured. When we got close, Grandma told Grandpa and me to run ahead and get the fire going real good and pull out the cradle and put a warm quilt in it. She said to milk the cow and heat the milk on the stove. We had to save this baby.

The baby fussed and fretted for a long time, it seemed, but then she accepted her new surroundings, and settled down. She stared at Grandma as if she was trying to figure out just who she was supposed to be. Her eyes searched the room, like she was wondering where her mama was. Grandma sent Grandpa to town with the word that we had the baby. She said to say that she seemed to be fine, but probably shouldn't be moved for two or three days. Grandpa said the Yankees questioned him kind of mean because they thought he knew who was behind the derailing of the train, but they finally said thanks. They would find out who the baby belonged to. Two days later a young lieutenant came to claim his baby. His eyes were red, and his face showed his grief as he walked stiffly and proudly up the steps to the porch. An older woman was in the wagon and she looked at our farm with a sour look on her face. The young father knelt down to the baby, and she gave him a questioning look. He stood up and thanked my Grandma for saving his child. He offered her some coins, but she said no, she would never take money for helping a child. "The only pay I want is for you to be good to the women and children you come across in this war."

The lieutenant's shoulders slumped a bit when she said that. I guess he was ashamed of the thoughts he'd been having. Then he straightened and said firmly, "Yes ma'am." I think he felt released from the burden of taking revenge.

The sour woman took the baby from the cradle and walked slowly to the wagon. The soldier helped her up, and the three of them settled in the seat. As the lieutenant turned the wagon back toward town, I ran beside it and asked the baby's name. He said, "We hadn't named her yet. We were waiting to be together to decide on a name."

I ran a few more steps and said, "Why don't you name her Bess? That's what I've been calling her."

He looked at me and smiled, "Bess? Maybe I will. Maybe I will."

***

I guess our family is luckier than most during this war. I don't think I ever went to bed hungry, but I know some children who have. Sometimes Grandma will hear of some family really suffering, and she'll pack up a basket for them. It may not be much—it may not have been the freshest or the best food God ever put on this green earth, but it would always be something that would help fill the belly. She'd say, "Grace, run this down to" so-and-so and I'd gladly oblige because it meant I could delay the other chores that weren't as much fun as a delivery. Sometimes, though, it wasn't so much fun when I got there, and the children would snatch the food out of my hands, eat it in about five seconds and look to me for more.

I'm not saying that we had too much, by any means. I didn't always get to have seconds. Sometimes Grandma didn't eat anything for supper, saying that she wasn't hungry. Now that I'm older, I wonder if she really had been.

Grandma said that before the war they had to work hard for it, but they always had food. Most of their neighbors did, too. If someone didn't have enough, the neighbors would likely be able to share something until the next crop came in, and they found nuts in the woods or killed some wild game. That's the difference. Now the neighbors don't always have enough to spare.

I try to help the best I can. Grandpa showed me how to fish, and sometimes I've brought home some whoppers, and my grandparents were so pleased. I've caught some crawdads that added a little meat to the meal that night. I've found blackberries and walnuts and dandelions which have tasty leaves. Grandma says that I can spy the best things because I'm low to the ground.

We don't go to town very often. It's not very close, so it's almost an all-day affair to get there and back before dark. Also, there are a bunch of Yankees there, and we try to steer clear of them. So mostly, we just stay on the farm. Sometimes, though, Grandma gets mad that this war has trapped her, and she says, "We've worked hard. We paid our taxes. We're going to town." So we give the animals extra food and water, and head to town all dressed up. It's a sad trip, really. Each time we go, we see more and more farms burned out. Fields that used to be bursting with crops or baby animals were empty now except for briars. Fences are gone because they've been used for firewood. The forests have been cut, so that now we only see stumps. We see more and more hungry eyes in the people walking along the road. Some are heading south, hoping life will be better where the Yankees haven't reached. Others are heading north to be with relatives who will take them in. Others are heading west to take their chances with the Indians. I look for hope, but I see little.

I asked my Grandma what this place was like before the war and she said, "Bountiful. It was filled with hard-working people. Lots of small farms that brimmed with large families. They made the land produce. It was all we needed."

We bounced along awhile and I asked, "Before the war, Grandma, was there as much killing?"

"Oh, no, dear. It was peaceful."

"Did you have men come in the night to scare you then?"

"No. It was law-abiding."

"Grandma, before the war, how many dead people had you seen that had been killed?"

She thought a moment. "Well, when I was a little girl, two men got into a fight over a woman. One killed the other. I didn't see it, but we went to the house where the dead man was laid out right there in the front parlor. Right before I met your Grandpa, our neighbor, who ran a prosperous store was robbed and killed on his way home one night. So, that's two."

I asked my Grandpa, "How many had you seen?"

"Honey," he said, "Ireland was a rougher place than Pennsylvania. I guess I've seen about twenty men killed there, over land or women or rent or just for saying a cross word. Here in America, though, I guess it was five before I met your Grandma. And no one since we married."

I pondered what they had said before I added, "I've already seen more killed people than you two ever saw before the war."

They didn't say anything, but they looked at each other sadly.

When we get near to the town, Grandma tells Grandpa not to fight back no matter what they say, and he promises. Once, though, *she* fought back, at least with words. Some Yankees were tormenting us, calling us nasty names which my

Grandma wouldn't want me to repeat, and Grandma spun around, grabbed one by the collar and said, "Would you want someone to talk to your mother that way?" That Yankee looked stunned and didn't say another word. As we walked away, my Grandma said, "What that boy needed was some well-placed shame." I guess she was right, because we never had any trouble out of him again.

I guess the Yankees were bored. They came down here to end slavery, or for adventure or because their friends joined up or because Abe Lincoln said they had to, and now they were standing around watching a bunch of people scratch the earth for a living. Or they got sent out to pick through the deserted farms or the ones run by women, children and old men, to take away what little those people had. I guess they expected something else. I guess everyone did.

I wonder what people did expect. I have been in some skirmishes with other children, although I hope my Grandma never finds out. I know that if you hit someone, they are going to hit back. I wonder why the leaders of both nations didn't know as much as that. I wonder if the people who thought this war was such a wonderful idea expected to see thousands of young men lying dead in a field. I wonder if they'd be surprised that nice Yankee ladies could find amusement by watching Northern boys put Southern boys on the wrong end of a fox hunt. I also would like to know whether they ever thought that a little farm girl like me could say I'd seen more people than hogs slaughtered, as the Confederate guerrillas and Union soldiers yanked the land back and forth.

This has become clear to me. No one knows what is going on anymore. No one knows what they are doing or why they are doing what they are doing. The other thing that is clear to me is that everyone wants to be home.

5

I asked my Grandpa why he never went to the war, or to any war for that matter. He got a distant look in his eye and said that every day in Ireland had been a battle—with the landlord or with the soil or with each other—fighting over the scraps the English didn't want. When he finally got out of there and came to America, he said he felt a yearning he couldn't explain. He just knew it couldn't be ended by fighting someone else's fight. So when there were battles with Indians or with Mexicans or whoever owned the land that the white folks wanted, he just kept walking. When he met Grandma he figured out what all the yearning had been for.

Somewhere between Ireland and Tennessee, he had lost his eye, and that's what kept him out of the war now. He wasn't sure even his age would keep them from riding up and saying he had to fight their war. But no eye, well, that was a different matter. He was fond of saying, "That's not bad, that's good." It took a while, but finally the loss of an eye turned into a good thing.

I'm glad he always got to stay with Grandma and find the piece of land they called their own. If he had been gone away like my Daddy, I don't know what my Grandma and I would have done. There were lots of farms with no men, and the women hitched the mules and scratched the earth and made some kind of living. But if the men had been there devoting themselves to the land like they devoted themselves to that war, well, it just would've been better.

My Grandpa's fine shooting provided us with many a meal. His sweat, like Grandma's, gave us vegetables and milk and more to eat. His presence at the table gave us comfort.

I asked Grandma if she minded that Grandpa would never be a war hero. "Not a bit. I'd rather have a warm body than a cold medal." I just nodded in agreement. "Men are given the choice of being a life taker or a life giver," she said. "Women don't have to make that choice."

"So Grandpa decided to be a life giver?"

"Yes, honey. That's right. That's why he's here."

"Which one is Daddy?"

Grandma looked sad. "I don't think we know yet."

I've got a friend, Paul Simpkins, who lives three farms away, and sometimes he comes over. He's not a boyfriend or anything like that, even though sometimes other kids tease me about that. It seems to be important to Paul to be better—

to get the biggest fish or climb the highest tree. Usually, he isn't better than me, though. After talking to Grandma, I started to wonder which he'll be—a life giver or a life taker. I hope he chooses what my Grandpa chose. I don't know that he will, though. Sometimes he'll take a stick and start whacking weeds and say, "That's what I want to do to those Yankees. I can't wait until I'm old enough to fight in the war."

I said to him, "Why would you want to leave when everything you need is right here?"

He wouldn't say anything. He'd just keep slicing the weeds. Then I'd say, "Why would you want to come back with one leg or no eyes or have to be carried around in a basket like the Shrum boy? Is that what you think is so great?"

Paul had stopped his great battle with nature, turned around and looked at me, mystified. "That wouldn't happen to me," he announced.

I wonder if that's what my Daddy thought. That he wouldn't be captured or lose his wife while he was away. That he would come back victorious, and all the throngs would greet him like Marc Antony.

"Why did Daddy leave us?" I asked Grandma. She dropped the socks she was knitting, and I could see her mind wandering elsewhere.

"He felt he had to go."

"Didn't he want to stay with me and Mama?"

"Yes, honey, he did."

I couldn't understand why he would go then. She looked at me sadly and said, "Child, his life wasn't his own."

That really puzzled me. He was grown with a room of his own and a little section of the land and a wife and child. Why wasn't his life his own? I learned later that people in Washington and then Richmond had put their brand on him, and his life would no longer be his, alone. Their decisions affected him and us, and we suffered every day because of it.

There was nothing to be done now, but to try to convince Paul that he should think before he signed up for something that didn't really concern him or that would make him leave his family. And I had to pray for my Daddy to come back to us. I had my work to do.

I wish that my Daddy hadn't been in a prison camp. The other men from this county that served in the army just kept sneaking home any time they wanted to see their families. They knew the land, having lived here all their lives. They got help from friendly farms along the way and got word where the Yankee patrols were. So whenever they got a pass and a notion, they'd come home for a visit. We learned a lot about the battles from them, more than the preacher learned from the newspapers. Once I was spending the night with a friend, Judy Littleton, when her Daddy popped up on the porch and scared us all half to death. Then the family erupted with joy. He hugged them all, even me, and danced his wife around. Then she said they'd better all go inside— you never knew who would spy them on the porch. It could have been a Union soldier. It could have been a neighbor loyal to the Union who wanted to gain the favor of the Yankees. Mr. Littleton scoffed, finding it hard to believe that one of their neighbors would turn them in, but she was firm. "You don't know what it's like here. You're on the battlefield. It's clear who your enemies are. Not here. A neighbor that will help you pull a cow out of a ditch one day will turn you in the next."

He looked at her sadly and I thought he was going to argue, but then picked her up, and said, "C'mon kids, your Mama has spoken," and carried her inside as she laughed. He twirled her around the kitchen, then set her down and said, "I'm starving. You got anything for an old weary soldier?"

Mrs. Littleton straightened her clothes and said, "Always."

I knew they didn't have much, but she made him a meal that would have made a king proud. She told him some of the funny things the children had done or said, and I could see he was right proud. He asked all the children if they had minded their Mama, and they all said yes. He laughed and said, "I thought you'd say that."

"How long can you stay, Tom?"

"I'll have to leave before dawn."

Everyone's smiles turned downward then. "Oh, Tom, I wish it could be longer."

"Me, too." He ate the rest of the meal in silence and asked, "How bad is it here?"

Before her husband got home, Mrs. Littleton had been saying she wasn't sure how they were going to make it through the winter, but she did not mention this to Mr. Littleton. She said later that she saw no reason to worry him. She told him that if they all worked hard, they would make it. I searched his eyes to see if he knew that she had not told him the truth, but I did not see it. Mr. Shakespeare says, "Frailty, thy name is woman," but I did not see any sign of weakness that night.

Mr. Littleton talked of the hardships of the war and told stories of valor which were so exciting, I wasn't sure the little ones would ever get to sleep. His oldest son asked him when the war would be over, and he said he expected that it would be soon. He said that they had fought hard, but he didn't see how the Southern army could fight much longer.

We all went to bed, and I cried thinking that I would not see my Daddy until the end of the war. Early the next morning before it was even light, I sensed stirring in the house and heard the Littletons say good-bye to each other. I did not hear Mrs. Littleton's tears until after her husband had gone.

Mr. Littleton sneaked home three more times, each time getting by the Yankee soldiers without a hitch. His boys took great pride in his being so wily. I'm glad he came home those times, for that is all the little ones remember about their father. He did not survive the war.

6

I've got a bunch of animals. Of course, they keep changing. The foxes get some of them. Soldiers on both sides help themselves. We have to eat some of our animals sometimes, so Grandma says not to get too attached.

I do, though. I remember the time Grandpa had to go and kill Shelby, my little goat. Grandma talked to me a long time and said we had to do it. I loved Shelby so much and I begged and begged for her life, so they put it off a few days. Grandma would bring up the subject, and I wouldn't hear of it. Finally she said that we were going to have to do it. We were running low on food, that's for sure. I pleaded for Shelby's life, listing all the other animals that should go first. I named Gladys the cow, but Grandma said that she gave us milk. I named Shelby's mean old mama, but Grandma said she gave milk, too. I named the chickens, but each one I named was a good egg layer. That got Shelby a week's grace, while we ate on a chicken or two. Then it reached the point that we had no more chickens to spare, not if we wanted any more eggs.

Grandpa got lucky and shot some squirrels, so Shelby saw the sun rise a few more days. Then I knew Shelby's last day had come. She and I walked the barnyard for the last time and I told her that she was the best goat anyone would ever hope to have. I think she told me that I was the best little girl that a goat could ever have. That sure pleased me. That's what I vow every Sunday before I fall asleep in church. To be the best little girl I can be.

I cried and cried as Grandpa set off with Shelby and a knife. He came back later, and Shelby was nothing but a cut-up carcass. That night we had meat on the table, but I only picked at it. I kept seeing my beloved Shelby and her pretty eyes. I can't say that Grandma and Grandpa ate much themselves. "Grace," Grandpa said. "I would have given anything not to have to have done that."

"I know, Grandpa." I never spoke of Shelby again. I think the worst thing Abe Lincoln ever made us do was to eat little Shelby.

Of course, we had cats and dogs. They were always having babies so we have plenty of them. Sometimes too many. Grandpa had to pack some up sometimes and take them to farms far away. The cats were helpful in keeping the rats down, but if one of those cats set its sights on a chicken that was the end of that cat. We sure didn't have enough chickens to share with the cats. The dogs were good about keeping away foxes, bobcats, and any other creature that might make off with one of our chickens, but sometimes one of our dogs would be caught with the goose feathers proudly coming out of his mouth and I'd have to say good-bye to that friend, too. We couldn't tolerate an animal that would eat General Albert Sidney Johnston.

Oh, I don't mean the actual general. Everyone knows he died at Shiloh. We never ran out of names for the animals, because I thought it was important to name them after Confederate generals. There was our black dog, General P.G.T. Beauregard. And the tabby cat, Stonewall Jackson. Of course, we have a Robert E. Lee. He's our rooster. Nathan Bedford Forrest, the hog, kept peace in our barnyard. Every time the preacher came with news of the war, he usually had the name of a new Confederate hero, and shortly afterward we'd have an animal that would proudly bear that name. Even birds that came to visit would leave with the name of a Confederate general. Sometimes their names were even longer than they were.

I wish the animals were more helpful with chores. They are mighty good about lying around and wondering what we're eating, but no help at all when it comes to candle making, soap making, canning and all the other chores that I have to help with because I know how to. Except when we have to eat them, or when they are the last ones to eat, I think they have the easier life.

Grandma is pretty good about letting me play, though. I know some children who are always working, and they get a whipping if they ever are caught doing anything else. Grandma gives me time to myself because I guess she knows that I need it. She calls me her "little thinker."

I do seem to need time to wonder. I wish I didn't have to do it so much and that I would just accept things the way they were. It seems like it would be easier. But I seem to need that time to sort out the troubles of our times.

We're lucky that we have a tiny cave not too far from our farm. I like to go in there and look at the pictures the Indians scratched on the walls. Every once in a while I find an arrowhead there and it gives me comfort because I know that years ago, an Indian stood in this same spot and looked out of this cave and saw the same beautiful sight that I see now. This place is so peaceful that it's a wonder that there is trouble anywhere. If only Lincoln and Davis could meet here, I think that everyone would be able to go home where they're supposed to be.

They say that there used to be elk and buffalo around here, but not anymore. Our skillets have to be content with deer, 'possum or squirrels. That is, if we're lucky.

Of course, if the war was over, that wouldn't get rid of all our troubles. We'd still have hail that rips through the corn, and fierce storms that make our kitten-soft river rage like a hungry hog. We'd still have wasps that sting, crafty raccoons that steal and mad skunks that stagger like they found some moonshine. Still, it seems that all the destructions of nature do not compare to the horrors that men can conjure up, even though the preacher's wife claims that people are God's rational creatures.

Sometimes Grandma worries that I think too much. "Honey, there are just some things that you can't figure out." Still, I think it is important to try. Some things I do believe that I know, and it's surprising to me that everyone doesn't—that parents and children should stay together. And that young men should not die because old men can't reach an understanding.

7

My Grandma was always collecting cloth remnants to make quilts, coats or anything that could keep someone warm. As soon as she was sure that Grandpa and I had enough clothes, she'd be making something for someone else. She would sell some eggs to get enough for postage, and then she'd mail the garment to Daddy. She wasn't sure he would get it, but she knew that someone who needed it would. If she couldn't get the postage, she'd take it to a poor family or to the preacher's wife to give to someone who needed it.

You see, no matter how little we had, I don't think that we knew that we were poor. We were just ourselves. And there was always someone else who had less.

I don't know how some families made it. They kept having children, but no place to put them, and no food to put in their mouths. Or, some families didn't have enough people to work the land. If Grandpa hadn't been so strong and determined, and if Grandma had been a dainty fancy woman,

I know that we wouldn't have made it. But they were hardened from years of toil and travel. They weren't about to lose the struggle with the land now. Not after all they had been through.

I thirsted for knowledge of my Mama. Grandma would say, "Honey, I've told you all I know. I wish her folks hadn't moved on. They could tell you more about her. How she was as a child. We didn't have her for very long."

"Can't we find them?"

"They were heading west. They didn't know how to read or write, and neither could we. So when they left, we all knew we'd never hear from them again."

I found that to be very sad. I wish they had waited a few years, because I would have made them promise that they would find somebody to write *me*.

"Then tell me about my Daddy."

Grandma never refused that request. She was very proud of her only child. "He used to catch snakes with his bare hands." She smiled and shook her head, then said, "Now don't you try that." She picked up her knitting again and continued, "There wasn't a tree he couldn't climb. That's where you get it," she said proudly. "Whenever I see you at the top of some tree, I don't bother to holler. It's in your nature."

I had to agree. The tops of trees were always calling to me.

"He loved to go down to the river and find a vine that would swing way out. He'd go flying out so far and sink so deep, I'd think, 'That's it. He's gone.' Then he'd come shooting up out of the water, laughing so hard that all my fear flew away. I'd tell him not to do that again. Of course, he would." She paused to soak in the happy memories. "He was such a good shot, that we always had meat on the table. Every night. Once he didn't get home until almost midnight, but he had a squirrel. It was the skinniest squirrel God ever made, but it was meat. I never had to worry when your Daddy was home."

Sometimes her voice would trail off and, even though I wanted to hear more about Daddy, I knew it was time to stop. I'd leave her alone with her memories and the tears that I knew would start soon. I'd go sit under a tree and pray and pray that my Daddy would come home to bring more meat home to Grandma.

I wonder what happened to my other grandparents. I hope they went a long way west, because I think that the war didn't go that far. I hope they own a lot of land, and the Indians leave their scalps on their heads, and they have lots of animals and food and that the rain is not too much or too little. I hope they learn to read and write so we can find out where they are. Maybe if they write, I can go see them, and if everything looks good, maybe Grandma and Grandpa and Daddy can all go live there and leave the war behind and never have to work again. I hope they write soon.

I wonder what Mama would have thought about not knowing where her parents were. Grandma said my Mama cried when they left, and asked them not to go. They said they had to. They just weren't making it on the farm. So off they went, and they never knew that they had two little granddaughters—me and then little Bess for a day.

I wonder why they don't get someone to write a letter for them. I hope it doesn't mean that they are dead, too. I don't want to think about that.

Old Lady Campbell lived across the river and three hills away, and Grandma sent me there with food when we heard that she was ailing. I didn't know why she would send me there, because they say that she killed and boiled a Yankee until he turned into soap when he said he was going to take her cow. Grandma says that didn't happen. I asked Old Lady Campbell why she thought my other grandparents don't let us know where they are. "Too busy living," was her short and sweet reply.

I asked her why the war was lasting so long.

"Too busy killing."

Old Lady Campbell lived alone, but I knew she had five sons and a husband. I asked her what happened to them and she said, "All dead." I kept staring at her, hoping that I'd get more details, but none came. So I had to ask Grandma.

"She keeps that grief to herself." Somehow I am not surprised.

The last time I went to see Old Lady Campbell, I took her some freshly baked cornbread. When I got to her farm, the cow looked swollen and confused, and the cats were complaining. I knocked on the door and, when I got no answer, I yelled for Old Lady Campbell. Still, she did not come. I pushed the door open, and the cold house told me something was wrong. She was sitting in front of the fireplace, but there was no fire to warm her. She was slumped over in her rocking chair like a nap had suddenly overpowered her.

I did not run in fright. I felt strangely at peace. This was how death was meant to be. It was supposed to come at the end of a long life. So it did not sadden me to see her there.

I found the bucket and milked the cow, which gave her some relief. I poured the milk over the cornbread to stop the cats from bawling. I found hay and grain for the cow, and slopped the hogs. When I was satisfied that the animals were cared for properly, I went to spread the news. I stopped at each farmhouse along the way and told them that Old Lady Campbell had left this world. Someone said they'd get the preacher. My Grandpa went to hitch up the wagon and get a shovel while I told Grandma. So many people came, and so many men were digging, that Old Lady Campbell had a grave in no time, despite the cold ground.

The preacher said a few words and then everyone discussed what was to be done with the farm and the livestock. As far as anyone knew, Old Lady Campbell had no living relatives. Somebody said that the land would go to the state, and everyone decided that was a bad idea. It was decided that the Durham family that was busting out of its cabin should have the farm. They were the ones most in need. They would send part of their family to live in Old Lady Campbell's cabin. Two sisters and their children had moved home when their men had gone to war. They were packed up along with their fourteen-year-old brother, and were expected to make their living. That left six children still at home. The Durhams thought they could manage better with that smaller number.

I went to visit the new Durham farm and saw that it continued on as before. They made use of everything that Old Lady Campbell had left behind. Except, of course, the soap.

8

Sometimes it's hard to know who your enemies are. Or your friends. Grandma says, "Maybe no one is either."

Now that the Yankees have taken over, Grandma does the same thing she has always done. She takes the little remnants that are not good enough to make clothes, makes bandages of them and takes them down to the church the Yankees use as a hospital. Same as always. Same as what she did when the Confederates ran this county. She said she didn't care where an injured boy was from. She would do what she could to help. Maybe she was hoping some mother would do the same thing for my Daddy when he made his journey home.

Well, you never heard such clatter. Helping out the Yankees! The very idea. People told her to stop. We even got mean night-visitors who told Grandpa he'd better control his wife. Grandpa knew better than to try. Women at church wouldn't speak to her. They cried about how those poor sick Yankee boys had put holes in their sons. They told her, "Don't shed tears for them."

That didn't stop Grandma. She kept doing it anyway. The only thing that stopped them was when she said, "What has this war turned you into? Has the Golden Rule turned to brass?"

She didn't just do good deeds for the Yankees. I don't want to leave you with that impression. No, she was committed to our cause, whatever that was. I guess it was the cause of surviving and helping her neighbors.

The news kept coming of battles and losses. More and more families shed tears. More of the Yankees that had been posted in our county were sent away. It became clear that the South had lost long before we got word that Georgia was being sliced in two by Sherman. Long before we got word that General Robert E. Lee had offered his sword in Virginia. I didn't consider it to be giving up, because that would be a bad thing. I'd say that it was like recognizing that it was time to salvage what was left and let brothers be brothers again. Time to let the army straggle home.

And they did. They passed through even our little section of the county, boys going both ways. We shared what we could, wishing them all a good journey. They looked tired, but hopeful that they could leave their bad memories behind.

We knew that this meant that Daddy would be making his way to us, that is, if he was still alive. I'd lie in bed at night, praying we'd see him soon. Praying that some sweet woman would give him an apple pie, and a kind man would say he could sleep in the barn just like he was the baby Jesus. I knew he'd be tired and hungry and eager to see us again.

I wonder if he thought of Mama while he walked. Of how she wouldn't be here to greet him like she was there to see him off. Grandma said Mama cried when Daddy left, but was proud of how handsome he looked in the uniform she had made for him. She had kissed him goodbye, and he had taken me from her arms and said to both of us that he'd be home before we even knew he had gone. I guess he was wrong about that. I don't remember his leaving, but I do have a sense of that scene. Maybe it's because I've asked Grandma to tell it to me so many times.

She said the cabin grew darker after he had gone. She couldn't explain it, because she knew the days had not instantly grown shorter, nor had the fire lost its glow. Yet, they all seemed to stumble as if they no longer could see their way. I wonder if Daddy had taken the light with him. Or, did no one have the light because the family was no longer together? Would it ever shine the same since my Mama wouldn't be here to combine her light with his?

These are the questions I pondered as I examined each man who made it to our door. I kept looking for that face from the picture that had grown so familiar to me. I did not see my Daddy, but I saw in these unshaven faces a similarity to one another. They were hardened by years of loss, and they each shared the kinship that came from stolen youth and stripped innocence. Still, they mustered a smile when they saw me. They'd say they had a daughter or a sister at home just like me, and that would inspire them to get up and keep going even though they were fighting exhaustion. That made me hope that my being here made Daddy walk a little faster.

I guess the reason that Grandpa didn't recognize Daddy at first was because he looked like so many of these soldiers who had come before. Maybe Grandpa had been afraid to hope that he'd see his son again. Maybe he expected more than a skeleton.

When I saw my Daddy, I wondered even more what the war had been about. At first, though, it was time to fatten him up and let him rest. We didn't exactly feast during the war, but we sure did better than Daddy. He was weak and tired. Still, the weeks at home didn't seem to help much. True, he was glad to be home, and he did love the good meals that Grandma managed to put together. Yet, he didn't seem to have the strength that he needed for the farm. Nor the strength necessary to deal with the women who swarmed looking for husbands among the leftover men.

I wondered if Daddy had forgotten how strong that he used to be. At least, that's how they used to talk about him. I thought maybe Daddy just couldn't remember how you had to work all the time on the farm. I saw how my Grandpa, who was a short man anyway, was sinking lower and lower on his spine, so I'd say to Daddy that some fence needed mending or some stump needed to be dragged here or there, expecting that he'd get up and do it. He'd say, "Thanks, honey," yet he didn't do the chore. In a few days, I'd see Grandpa up there taking care of the problem, never saying a word to Daddy about the days that he spent staring. Sometimes I'd catch him holding something of Mama's, and I'd see him cry, but I'd never let on that I'd seen. Sometimes

I'd see him up on the hill, rubbing his hands over little Bess' tombstone. I guess he talked to her just like I do.

I began to realize that the hardest thing for Daddy was not the war. It was having to come home to the knowledge that Mama wasn't here anymore. Maybe it was easier in a prison camp to pretend she'd still be there with her smile and her kisses. To put a plate of steaming food in front of him at night and to tell him she loved him and that he was the best husband and father that had ever lived. Now he could feel too clearly the loss her death had brought.

I wondered how different he would have been if my Mama had been alive. I pictured her dropping everything just like Grandma, and running to grab him. I pictured him sweeping her up in his arms and me, too, and swinging us around as if we weighed no more than kittens. We would have been so happy to see each other, and I know that we would have gotten through all the hard times a lot better.

But that was not to be for us. Our days were filled with hoping that Daddy would return to us in soul as well as body. As hard as the early days after his return were for him and for us, I guess we all would welcome back those days that Daddy dragged himself through. Because any contentment that we knew came to an end when we received that letter from that Illinois Yankee.

9

We have a corn field that is so high up the hill, it's almost straight up from our cabin. That's where I was playing when I heard Grandpa call for me. "Grace. Hey, Grace. Come here," he bellowed. I dropped the corn husks and stalks I was playing with and ran down to him. I knew he wanted me real bad, so I considered sliding straight down the hill, but thought the better of it because I was wearing a dress with no holes in it. It had to be important, because he didn't often call for me. Once I was done with my chores, he let me be. I should say that once I had done my chores right, he let me be.

I knew something unusual was happening because when I reached him, he grabbed my hand, and we hurried to the cabin wordlessly.

I had to walk three steps for his one, but I never said a word. I wondered if I had done something wrong and thought back over the last few weeks to think of the things I had accidentally torn up and hidden, or of chores I had halfway done, hoping to have a chance to come back to them. I couldn't think of anything that would cause this much to-do.

Grandma and Daddy were on the front porch, obviously waiting for me to get there. *Uh-oh*, I thought. *I'm going to get it now.* As we got closer I saw that Grandma was holding something in her hand. I wondered what I could have done to that thing. Then, I felt better. It looked like a letter. I bounded up on the front porch and she handed it to me. "Grace, read us this letter," Grandma said.

I was shaking when I took it in my hands, even though I realized that I wasn't in trouble for anything. The outside of the letter gave a man's name and address: Bertram Manning, Spring Street, New City, Illinois. Then it said: *To the family of the woman who disappeared February 1863, East Branch of Bledsoe Creek, Bransford, Tennessee.*

I was shocked just by the address. So was my family. I didn't make any move to open the letter, and no one asked me to for a few minutes. You see, when no one would talk to me about where my Mama was, I had stopped asking. I had the manufactured memories my Grandma had given me from the happy stories she told, but I can't say that I had a real memory of my Mama. But that address gave me a vague stirring in my mind that maybe I did know something of my Mama on my own. I began to remember tears—the tears of my Grandma that I had seen so often.

"Grace," Grandma said gently. "Open the letter. It's time we know." My Daddy walked to the edge of the porch and clutched the railing so tightly I thought he would break it.

Grandma started to rock back and forth rapidly in her chair. Grandpa slowly sat down on the steps of the porch as I began. Until that moment, I never thought of Grandpa as an old man.

The letter was dated November 13, 1866, and began simply enough. "I was a Union soldier, stationed in Gallatin, Tennessee. I was a private, and it was my duty to go out from time to time to find provisions and be sure that there was order." I swallowed hard and looked at my Grandma. I had stumbled on a few of the words.

"Go on, dear," Grandma urged. "Do the best you can."

I returned to the letter. "On one of these days in the fall of 1862 we came upon a pretty young woman beside Bledsoe Creek. She was there gathering some delicate flowers, singing a soft song and holding a little girl in her arms." *That would have been me*, I thought. "We watched her for awhile, and listened to the sweet singing but didn't bother her. It was a peaceful scene that helped us forget the war.

"A few weeks later we were sent to the same area again and we thought we'd try to get another glimpse of her. I think we five soldiers had built her up into something she wasn't— someone who would look upon us with favor. We forgot the war and the fact that she probably had a man and family. What would she want with us? That, we did not stop to consider. We were young and lonely and, even though we had superiors, there was really nothing to stop us from doing anything we wanted.

"This time, instead of being able to watch her from afar and keep a peaceful scene, we stumbled upon her and frightened her. She didn't believe us when we said we meant no harm. She was not the loving creature we had envisioned. She yelled, called us names, and fled from us.

"We followed her to her cabin, but we left again. Still, we were haunted by her beauty. As we talked, we made ourselves angry that we were not at home where we wanted to be, trying to get our own beauties to pay attention to us. We were hurt that this beautiful creature did not want us. Did not want to comfort us or cook for us or welcome us into her home. We were angry that her man was probably killing our soldiers on the battlefield, and she'd probably kill us, given half the chance.

"I am cursed by what we did next. War makes it easy to hurt, but hard to forget. I don't know if there is any redemption for what we did. I do not know if this letter will help you, or if you would rather not know. I tell myself that I write this letter for you, but I must confess that I am writing it to try to find my own peace—the peace that does not come simply from the laying down of arms.

"After we had convinced ourselves that this young woman had wronged us in some manner, and after we added liquor to the recipe, we went looking for this woman. We found her cabin and sat and waited.

"An old man came out and went to tend his animals. We stayed silent. A little girl came out and jumped around the porch, but the old man took her in with him. We still just watched. Then, just when we were about to give up, the young woman came out. Oh, how I have wished she had never left the cabin that night.

"But she did, and for that I must pay all my days. She walked out the door and down the lane. I heard her say, 'Oh, William, when are you coming back to me?'"

I stopped my reading then, because my Daddy had started to cry. My Grandma got up from her rocking chair and took the letter from me. "Grace, honey, run to find the preacher."

"Aren't we going to finish the letter?"

"The preacher can finish it for us."

"I can read it."

My Grandma looked at me kindly. "I know, dear, but there are some things you're too young to hear."

I didn't argue, because I knew my Grandma's mind was made up. Before leaving, I ran up to Daddy and gave him a kiss. I told him that everything was going to be all right. He looked at me and did not say a word. I didn't think he believed me.

The sadness stood between us, and neither of us said another word. I called for General P.G.T. Beauregard, who had come near to listen to the letter and to scratch. He struggled to his feet, stretched, and we ran off to get the preacher.

10

It wasn't easy to find the preacher. Sometimes he'd be out on his circuit so he wasn't anywhere nearby. Of course, even when he was in our area, he was ministering to the sick or the afflicted or the poor. That's what the Bible said to do and that is what he did. I never heard him say a word of complaint about this life he had chosen. Or the life that had chosen him.

So this time when I had to find the preacher, I had to run from farm to farm, searching for a word of him. The preacher's wife was not at home, but the Greenfields thought he was at the Benton farm. The Bentons said he had been there yesterday, but had left. They thought he was at the Franklin farm. I ran and ran, not even stopping to do an inspection of a beaver's home or hornets' nests. My chest and legs ached so, but still General Beauregard and I kept running because we knew that was the only way we would find out what happened to Mama.

As you know, I've often wondered why I had no Mama. I guess any child would have. These days, there were lots of children who had no fathers. There are plenty of dead heroes, though. Most of them seemed to be able to scrape up a mother. Maybe she wasn't too pretty, or blessed with much sense, but still she was their blood, and she took care of them the best she could.

So you can see that I would feel a loss, even though I had the best grandmother in the world. Many a night I've said a prayer of thanks for her, and I don't have any complaints, even though she has spanked me a time or two. Still, though she tried hard, I always knew that there was someone called Mama who was supposed to take care of me, but didn't for very long. That's why I ran as long and as hard as I did, because I felt I was going to get back part of my Mama.

I found the preacher at the fifth farm I was sent to, and I must have looked a fright, because at first his face showed the fear of someone who was about to be given the bad news of a death. When I explained that we had gotten a letter about my Mama, his face lifted a bit, but the graveness returned when he looked at me and said kindly, "Yes, Grace, I will come. Give me a moment."

He went back in the house, and I heard him talking to the family in need. The woman came out with a cup of milk and a piece of cornbread, and I thanked her for them. General Beauregard and I drank and ate in a hurry, because I was anxious to get back to the news of my Mama.

The preacher finally was finished, and he put his foot in the stirrup and hoisted his large frame onto the back of his horse.

He reached out his hand for me, and I put my little hand in his. In one swift tug, he pulled me behind him, and we were off, with General P.G.T. Beauregard leading the way home. At first, we were riding at a good clip; then he slowed his horse's pace. "Grace, I never knew your mother," he said.

"Brother Carson, I don't think *I* did."

"Oh, I'm sure you knew her. Part of you still remembers her. Blood always knows." The preacher paused while the horse plodded along. Then he continued, "Grace, I don't know what is in the letter. But it could be really bad, so bad that you can't be told about it until you're much older. I want you to remember, though, that there were people who loved your Mama very much, that she was a good, decent woman who loved you and your father. Never lose sight of that, no matter what clutter and horrors other people have brought to your family."

The horse trotted right along as I said, "I won't, sir."

When we approached the house, my family came onto the front porch, and I could see they were much relieved to see us. I looked around the farmyard, and even though I figure I'd been gone over two hours, not one single thing was different. No one had done a lick of work. That concerned me as much as anything. We were a family of workers, and so far, even Daddy's capture by the Yankees had slowed the chores only for a small part of a day.

My Grandpa came to the horse and lifted his arms to me. I reached forward and he took me off the horse with his strong, steady arms. The preacher dismounted and walked up the steps to the porch, removing his hat. "I hear you folks have gotten some news."

"Yes, preacher," said my Grandma.

"It would be my honor to read the letter to you."

"Thank you, preacher," said my Grandpa.

I saw the letter on the rocking chair and picked it up. "Look, preacher. This is where I stopped." I handed it to him.

"Grace, honey, I want you to go to the barn and collect the eggs," my Grandma told me.

"Grandma, I want to hear the letter."

"Don't argue with your Grandma," my Daddy snapped.

I was shocked because my Daddy had not displayed anything but sadness since his return. I started to say that I'd get the eggs later, that there probably weren't that many since I'd just gathered some the first thing that morning, but I didn't say another word. I slowly walked down the steps to the barn. I kept looking back to see if Grandma had changed her mind. I saw the preacher reading to himself up to the point where I had left off, I guess. I ran to the barn, then. I gathered up the eggs faster than lightning strikes and went out the door on the far side of the barn. I ran through the woods, came up behind the cabin and crawled up underneath the porch. I didn't care how dirty I got, or if I put the first hole in my dress. I could hear every word as the preacher began to read.

I learned what happened to my Mama during the short time that the preacher read. Almost harder, I had to pretend I didn't know. I had plenty of questions, particularly why it all happened to someone as sweet as my Mama was said to be. Why didn't God protect her if he's supposed to care about us more than those lilies in the field? Did she have to go because little Bess needed her Mama? Was she taken because I wasn't a good enough girl? Had I committed one of those bad sins the preacher is always talking about?

I wish I could have asked these questions of the preacher, because I think he's supposed to know. I had to keep my silence, though, because I'd be in trouble if they knew that I'd heard what had happened to my Mama.

The Bible says the truth shall set you free. I guess that means that some questions get answered. Some of the darkness disappears. But does the truth help keep you from being blinded by the light? I don't know.

11

As I was hiding underneath the porch, General Beauregard joined me and gave me all the comfort that a dog's licking could bring. He knew something was wrong, but wasn't quite sure what it could be. Stonewall Jackson did some licking, too, but mostly of herself. She's a very clean cat and took the news about my Mama quite calmly.

The preacher started where I had left off.

"We didn't give her any more time to wonder about when her William was coming home. We were angry that she wasn't wondering when *we* were coming to see her. We each took one more drink; and one of us grabbed her. I don't know who. She never had a chance even to scream. We dragged her through the woods to our horses, flung her across a saddle, and we were gone.

"At the time it seemed like grand adventure. Her fear didn't matter. Impressing each other with our brutality did. If I had remained at home under my mother's watchful eye, I know I never would have done such a thing. Alone, away from preachers and family, with no law except the law of strength, I was a beast. No, worse than a beast, because I should have known better. Years of guidance and love should have stopped me.

"I should not have done it. Better yet, I should have stopped it. I never said a word against it. That would have been strength, but I didn't have it.

"We kidnapped her; we took our turns with her; we killed her. We laughed about it. We hid her body and pretended that we didn't do it. One of us was even assigned to help look for her when the general ordered a search for the missing woman. We knew that she wouldn't be found. Even if her body had been found, we knew they wouldn't do anything to us. After all, wasn't she the enemy?

"We escaped punishment then, but not ultimately. For when the war ended and reality returned, I went home to my family. They were so glad to see me, so proud I had fought for my country. They said how noble I was to fight to end slavery. I was treated like a hero, although I knew I was a horror.

"Before the war, I thought I had felt the call. After things settled down, my mother asked me if I still thought I wanted to be a preacher. At the time, she didn't understand the look of shame on my face, or why I left that night and didn't return until someone dragged me home, drunk and unconscious. When I woke up and realized I was home, I was horrified. I cried that night, as my mother did after she guessed what I had done. I should have known I couldn't hide it from her any better than I could have hidden it from myself.

"Since that night, I have been haunted by my mother's look of disappointment. All her hard work, and this is what she produced. The sweet boy who brought her flowers, who told her that he loved her, and that she was pretty, had committed monstrous acts with little prompting. I know that I have dishonored all who loved me and raised me and sacrificed so much for me.

"Your dear one has not been silent since the night I helped kill her. She has visited me in my dreams often, sometimes with looks of judgment. Surprisingly, sometimes she comes with looks of kindness. Any look was my damnation. I cannot see a little girl without thinking that I have robbed one sweet girl of her mother.

"That is what happened. You will find her body beneath a giant sycamore one mile east of the bridge that crosses Bledsoe Creek. There is a chimney, all that remains of an old farmhouse, and a decayed barn that still has the smell of tobacco. A tilted horse trough is beside the door to the barn.

"Now you know the truth. I do, too. Even though I have known what I have done, until the moment I put this in writing, it did not seem real. Still, I must accept it and any consequences that come from this letter. You have this letter. You will soon have her remains. You know where I live and my name. I don't know if the authorities will do anything to me. Probably not. I don't know if anyone will come for me, but I am prepared for you. I hope that punishment in this world will result in mercy in the next. Of course, I know I don't deserve something as pure as mercy.

"I expect that this letter has caused you much pain. I hope, though, that you can forgive me in some way, because I cannot forgive myself."

The preacher paused at this point. Then, he finished, "It is signed, 'Bertram Manning.'"

I waited for my family's reaction or some words of comfort from the preacher. I heard soft sobbing, but no one said a word. I noticed that my own face was wet, but I did not dare make a sound. I silently crawled out from beneath the porch, ran back through the woods and was in the barn by the time my Grandpa got there.

I hurriedly dried my tears and said, "Here, Grandpa. I got all the eggs."

"That's good, honey." Grandpa was pulling out his ax and saw.

"What are you doing, Grandpa?"

"I'm going to cut a tree and make a coffin."

"For my Mama?"

"Yes, Grace. For your Mama." He finished gathering together everything he would need, and turned to me and said, "Grace. Come with me. I want you to pick out the tree."

He didn't need to ask me twice. I said, "Yes, Grandpa," and off we went with the sway-back mule. I selected a gorgeous oak and he told me to stand back. He slammed that ax into the tree real viciously and I knew that he was doing to that poor tree what he wanted to do to those bad men. My Grandpa was old, but he was scrappy, and the tree did not have a chance. It was down and the branches cleared off in no time at all. My Grandpa was drenched in sweat and I was, too, from hauling all the branches we didn't need. It was almost dark by the time we got the tree dragged back to the barn.

We ate a quick silent supper, and then my Grandpa went back to the barn to begin work on the coffin. I watched him for awhile and then started back to the cabin. I stopped in the darkness when I heard my Grandma say to my Daddy, "You're going, aren't you?"

"Yes."

"Forget about revenge, son. You've got a daughter to raise."

"It's something I've got to do."

"What do you intend to do? Walk up and murder him?"

"It wouldn't be murder. It would be justice."

"The only justice you will see will be the inside of a jail. If you're lucky. You don't think his family will just sit there while you walk up and kill their son, do you? When it comes down to dying, don't think that soldier will be willing to go. He'll fight you. That's his instinct. Let him live with his guilt. Maybe that is punishment enough."

"He needs to feel the hell I feel."

"Maybe he does feel it, son. Maybe he does."

My Daddy didn't have anything to say to that, at least for a while. Then, he said, "I can't forget she lived. I can't forget how she died. Don't I dishonor her if I do nothing? What would she say if I did nothing?"

"I think she'd say, 'Think of the living. Raise my daughter. There's been enough killing.' That's what I think she'd say. If you go up there to kill, you're doing it for yourself. Not for her."

My Daddy left the front porch and went into the cabin. A few minutes later I joined my Grandma on the front porch. I was glad when she patted her lap, and I sat down on it. As she rocked, I knew she was thinking about what to tell me about my Mama, but I did not dare encourage her for fear that I would give away that I already knew it all. Still, I was about to burst. There were some words that I didn't know their meaning. I wasn't clear on some of the things that happened to Mama. Then I got to worrying that my Grandma would be suspicious if I didn't ask any questions, since she knows I'm a wonderer. Finally, I said, "Grandpa is building a pretty coffin for Mama."

"Yes, he is. That man does fine work."

"Grandma? Are you going to tell me what the rest of the letter said?"

"Grace, I don't believe in lying to children, but I don't believe in putting too much of a burden on them, either. You can understand that, can't you?"

"Yes, ma'am."

"We worried and wondered what happened to your Mama. We were about sick over it. Now we know. But what I think you need to know now is that your Mama is dead, which we all knew. She was a good woman, a good mother. A delight. She was taken from this world too young. I don't want you to dwell on that, though. I want you not to think of the evil in this world, honey, because there is plenty of that. You don't have to look too hard or far for that." She rocked some more before she continued, "Look for the good. *Be* good. That's what your Mama would have wanted."

We rocked for a good while in silence. Then Grandma told me it was time to go to bed. I went inside to get ready, and saw that my Daddy was packing to leave. I was hoping my Grandma's wisdom would keep him here, but I saw that it would not. My Daddy would not look me in the eye when I said, "You going somewhere, Daddy?"

"Yes, Grace," he said as he cleaned his rifle.

"Why, Daddy? You just got home. You have to leave again so soon?"

He still didn't look up, but he did slow his cleaning for a moment. I wanted him to drop his rifle and give me a hug, but he didn't. He grasped it tightly and said, "I hope someday you'll understand that it's something I have to do."

I stared at him for a minute or two, still hoping for some understanding between us, still hoping that he would choose raising me over revenge, but he did not. I think, and hope, he felt the shame of it. I knew he was searching for honor and peace, but where is the honor in leaving children? How could that bring peace in his soul, when it troubled mine so? If his leaving could have brought back my Mama, I would have wanted him to go. But his leaving would only mean *he* would be gone from me, too. I couldn't understand why he couldn't see that.

The next day he walked away. And so, even though the history books are going to say that the war ended in 1865, I know that it is a lie. The war continued for us as my Daddy left to fight demons, in his head and out in the world. And we continued to wait for bad news as we had done already for so many years before. Waiting for men to figure things out wears me out.

12

Over the next few weeks, we tried to live our normal lives, at least as normal as a heavy weight would allow. Grandma was a little snappish. I cried for no reason at all. Grandpa stayed late in the fields and said little at meals. As I watched them worry, I began to believe that there was something worse than losing a son. That would be losing a son you didn't have to lose.

Finally, when it was almost time to think about another Christmas without my Daddy, we saw the preacher coming. In his hand was another letter. When my Grandma saw him, she clutched her heart and collapsed in the rocking chair. She knew that this was the bad news she had been dreading for so many years. She started to cry before the preacher even got the letter open.

The preacher looked over the letter and grasped my Grandma's hand tightly. "It is not what you think. He's alive."

Grandma said, "Praise God. I still have a son."

"Yes," said the preacher. "I think you'll be proud." He read on, then his face turned a bit gray. "Perhaps not."

"Not yet, preacher," my Grandma said. She told me to run to get Grandpa and I was off the porch before she finished the instruction. General Beauregard and I completed our mission quickly. I yelled to Grandpa that Daddy was alive and we had a letter. Grandpa dropped the ax where he stood and hurried back with us.

When we returned, I could tell that Grandma and the preacher had been talking about whether I should hear the letter. "Please, please," I begged.

Grandma looked to the preacher. "Is it bad?"

"Part of it is bad, but she's entitled to know her father," was the preacher's judgment.

Grandma rocked a moment. "Grace, you can stay."

The preacher began by saying, "It's from Bertram Manning." I knew then that Daddy had not killed him. The preacher started to read. "Mr. and Mrs. Meadows, your son arrived here December 1. I felt his presence even before I heard that someone had been asking for me. I didn't try to hide, though I did think of it. I saw a man walk back and forth in front of my house for about an hour and I knew he had come for me. Finally he came to the door. After he knocked, I opened the door, but could not look him in the eye. He asked me if I was Bertram Manning. I was tempted to lie, just like I was tempted to run, but I did not. I said, 'Yes, I am.' The next thing I knew, I was getting the beating of my life. He thrashed and kicked me. All the time, I did not resist. I was spitting blood, and could hardly see him when he stopped and reached for his rifle. By then, the neighbors had come out and I heard one of them tell him to stop. I yelled at them to shut up. That your son had every right. I looked up at your son as he raised the rifle to my face and I knew that I was about to die just as I deserved. I felt a strange peace.

"Then something happened that I will never forget. The rifle started to shake and your son started to cry. He lowered the rifle. I started to cry, too, and I begged him to kill me. We both sat in the dust, two brave soldiers, two former enemies, now two brothers, united by our sins.

"You see, Mr. and Mrs. Meadows, he was crying because he, too, had committed unspeakable acts. I think that we are human again, because we have confessed our sins and know we need forgiveness.

"He spent several nights with my family, and he and I talked over the war as we have talked to no one else. I think he thought I would understand because of the burden I carried. There is innocent blood on my hands, as on his, but some of the innocent blood he spilled must be pooled at my feet. You see, he did what he did after he learned that his wife was missing.

"I want you to know that your son is a good and decent man, not only because he spared my life when I didn't deserve it, but because he has gone to make amends to the family *he* has harmed. He said he must do it before he will feel whole and be able to return to his own family, if God allows.

"What your son did was this: He was understandably quite upset to learn that his wife was missing and probably dead. The loss of his infant daughter, Bess, the long separation from little Grace and his beloved wife, watching senseless slaughter, well, it was too much to learn that he would never see his wife again. She hadn't wanted him to go to war, as I am sure you knew, but he felt he had to. By the time he learned she was missing, he had forgotten his reasons for fighting, and wanted only to be with her. Now he could never have that again.

"He had the guilt of knowing he had left her alone, and he had to live with the fact that he had not been there to protect her. The anger over his life grew and grew and was not helped by the harsh conditions of the battlefield.

"One day when he was sent out to find provisions, he discovered a young Union soldier who had fallen asleep. It would have been easy to keep going and leave the poor boy there, or to capture him and take him back with him. Instead, he put a rifle to the boy's head, took the boy's gun, kicked his boot, and asked him if he was ready to die. The boy yelled, 'No!'

"Your son said, 'Yes!' and pulled the trigger, imagining that boy was the one who killed his wife. You know, that boy could have died in any number of battles, but of course, that doesn't matter. His blood was on your son's hands then.

"After he killed him, your son took his boots, his rifle, anything he could find that he could sell or use. He went through his pockets and discovered a letter and a picture of a young woman. He said he once wished he had left those behind, although now he is thankful he did not. A day or two later, he found someone who could read, and learned that the young man's wife, Susan, had just written him to say she was going to have a baby. As soon as your son could get a little distance away from the other soldiers, he said that he broke down and cried.

"That's been the burden he's been carrying—that he didn't kill because he was ordered to, or because someone was trying to kill him, or for some cause that none of us can now remember. He killed a man that he didn't have to kill, for no other reason except that he was in pain.

"He's gone to a small town near Dayton, Ohio, to ask for forgiveness and to see if he can help the young widow and child. I hope that you will soon see your son again and that he will again be as whole as possible in this world of war. If you do not see him again, I hope you can be proud of him, for I can tell you that it is a brave man who can face the ones he has wronged and say, 'Forgive me.' I would rather face a thousand cannons than do it again. And it is a strong man, when faced with someone who has wronged him, who can say, 'I forgive you.' Your son has done both."

The preacher looked up from the letter and saw that there was nothing else to say at this time of relief and bewilderment. "I'll be going now, Mr. and Mrs. Meadows. Let me know if you need anything." I walked the preacher to his horse.

"Will my Daddy go to hell now, preacher?" I asked fearfully, for I knew now that he had broken one of the big commandments and couldn't hide behind the excuse of war or battle or that Jeff Davis said he should do it.

The preacher knelt down and gave me a hug. "Grace, I think your father's going to work his way out of his hell."

I was grateful for his words. I spent the rest of the afternoon wondering if the widow and her family would be as forgiving as my Daddy had been. I sure wish my Daddy had learned to write. I thought he might fare better by letter than in person. Why didn't that Bertram Manning write a letter for him? That's the least he could have done, since he killed Mama and all.

I wished we'd never gotten any letter, and Daddy was still here moping around, keeping his secret to himself. I didn't want to know that my Daddy had done anything wrong. I had preferred that he be some great warrior, fighting for right, whatever that was. I didn't want to know that he was a scared, hurt little man, lashing out just for the sake of it.

I said to Grandma, "I don't understand why Daddy did what he did."

She stopped her scrubbing and said, "Honey, I don't think even your Daddy understands. He's a better man than that story will ever lead you to believe." She started scrubbing again. "If only they had left him alone."

They tell me that women don't have the right to vote. I guess that's because if they were asked, "Is it okay if we take your sons from you and kill them or turn them into animals?" they would say, "No, thanks." I wish someone would ask me what *I* thought. If someone asked me if Daddies should stay home or go kill each other, I'd say, "Stay home." It seems simple enough. Today, if someone asked, I'd vote for my Daddy to come home. Trouble is, no one ever does.

13

While we waited for more news of my Daddy, Grandpa went up the hill to Bess' grave and dug another one beside it. The next morning before any of us even woke up, he left with the wagon and the coffin. He found his way to that sycamore tree that Mr. Manning had described. He said that he followed the directions and had no trouble at all. I had wanted to go with him when he went, to help him bring home the remains of my Mama. They both had said no, that Grandpa would go alone. I knew that they would say that.

I went about my chores, but kept waiting to hear the clanking of the wagon or the snorting of the sway-back mule that would be the sign that my Mama was home. As soon as I heard those noises, I dropped what I was doing (thank goodness I wasn't gathering eggs at the time) and ran to the wagon. I don't know what I was expecting. The coffin looked the same as when Grandpa left. I asked if she was in there, and Grandpa said, "Yes, honey, there's your Mama's earthly remains."

"Can I look at her?" You see, I hoped she was still as beautiful as everyone said she was.

Grandpa said firmly, "No, honey, you can't."

Grandpa stopped in front of the horse trough and got off the wagon just as Grandma came out of the house. She didn't say a word as Grandpa washed off the outer layers of his dirt. I saw him pick up his razor and shoo away from the mirror the bird that comes every day to peck at its own image. I never understood why that bird couldn't figure out that it could not win that war.

When Grandpa and I made it to the house, Grandma said, "Wash up now. Put on your Sunday clothes." Grandpa went to the table and quickly ate the plate of beans she had waiting for him. Then he went to their bedroom. By the time I had brushed my hair and was all dolled up, Grandma and Grandpa were all dressed up, too.

I guess Grandpa had seen the preacher on his way back to us, because just then the preacher and his wife pulled up in their wagon. They both smiled, but not too much, considering this was a solemn occasion. Grandma got her Bible from the mantel, and she and I got into the wagon with the preacher. The preacher's wife took my hand and patted it the whole time that we rode up the hill to the grave. No one said a word as we went. The birds singing, the grasshoppers buzzing and the wheels grinding through the ruts were the only sounds that joined us. The way got steep, and we had to hold on to keep from falling backwards onto the wagon. It's even hard just to walk, and the mule and the preacher's horse had to strain to get us there. Finally, Grandpa stopped the wagon beside the freshly dug hole, and he and the preacher struggled to get the coffin into the grave. They lowered it with ropes, and it came to rest on the bottom with a thud.

It seemed strange that we should be having this service without my Daddy. I said so to Grandma, and I could tell she agreed by the way she pursed her lips. She said, "We'll have another service when he comes back." That made me feel a little better, but I bet Mama and Little Bess are wondering where he is.

The preacher began the service. "We are here to pay tribute to Estelle Meadows. Loving wife and mother. Beloved daughter-in-law." At that point, I buried my head in Grandma's dress and began to cry. The preacher continued, "The good Lord never made a better person than Estelle, and she is sorely missed by her loved ones. We take comfort, though, in knowing she is with her Lord and her little girl. We will meet her in the hereafter where all the sorrows of this world will be gone and we might be able to understand God's mysterious ways." The preacher reached down and picked up some dirt and threw it on the coffin. All of us did the same. Only I added a pretty pink flower to the mix.

My Grandma sang "Softly and Tenderly, Jesus is Calling." As her voice reached the high notes of "Ye who are weary come home," my spirit soared with it and I felt my Mama had found some peace. While the preacher and Grandpa stayed behind to fill in the grave, Grandma, the preacher's wife, and I made our way silently down the hill. I walked between them holding their hands. I was going to ask questions to see if it would help make sense of it all. But I didn't. I had decided by then that it all made no sense, and that adults knew little more than children about why things turned out the way they do.

14

After my Mama was laid to rest, I became very sad. I kept waiting for my Daddy to come home, but he did not. I now knew my Mama would never come back to me, no matter if I was a good girl for the rest of my days. My Grandma tried to cheer me, even though I knew she was feeling the weight of sadness herself.

The preacher's wife began to be worried about me, and I could tell she was trying to figure out what she could do for me. One day she came to visit my Grandma, and I was sent to gather eggs, again! The preacher's wife left, and I wondered what all that had been about. Later, I heard Grandma talking to Grandpa, and then I learned what the preacher's wife wanted.

She was going to Nashville for two weeks or so, and wanted to know if I could go with her.

To Nashville! I said *yes* I could go, but I regretted saying it so soon, because I could tell it hurt my Grandma's feelings by saying so quickly that I wanted to do it. I added, "If you think you and Grandpa can do without me."

Grandma smiled and said, "Honey, we'll be all right. If it's what you want to do."

I decided to make her feel better by saying that I would miss her and Grandpa, and she seemed pleased with that.

"It's just that the preacher's wife thinks that this trip will be good for you. That you shouldn't be sitting around thinking about your Mama so much," my Grandma explained.

I was a little bothered by that, because wasn't I always supposed to remember my Mama? But I didn't say that. I said, "Yes ma'am."

So it was settled. I was going to see a big city, much bigger than anything I had ever seen in my life. There would be fine ladies and fancy-dressed gentlemen with manners and everything. There would be more to do than chores and worrying about where Daddy was or if he was still alive.

Grandma let me run to tell the preacher's wife that I could go, and I think she was as thrilled as I was. She said that we wouldn't be leaving for about a month. While we waited, we needed to get ready. She said she wanted to teach me some of the table manners that we hadn't bothered with yet. She told me that she needed to go to Nashville to help her father develop a plan for teaching the Negro children to read.

I panicked when she said that. "You aren't going to leave us, are you?"

She smiled and patted my head. "I have no plans to leave. My father needs to hear about the best way to proceed in the rural counties. You see, he's lived all his life in the city. He's been put in charge of Middle Tennessee and wants to do a good job. Also, I haven't seen my parents for several months. It's time we got together."

I was greatly relieved at the news that my beloved teacher would not be moving away. I decided to watch her closely while in Nashville to make sure she didn't get a hankering to return to city ways.

The preacher's wife and I talked about which fork to use when, and curtseys that looked good and those that looked awkward. We worked on my "yes ma'am's" and "no ma'am's" and, as the preacher's wife put it, "how to look interested even when someone is a bore." That was going to be the hardest part of pretending to be a lady.

My Grandma worked hard getting a new dress ready for me, and mending another. My Grandpa sold a pig to get money for new shoes. The preacher's wife gave me an old purse that had beads and everything. When it came time to go to Nashville, I was as shiny as a lathered-up black horse, and as refined as twice-ground corn meal.

The night before we were to leave, Grandpa took me over to spend the night with the preacher's wife. The train was leaving early the next morning and there was no way to make it from our farm without starting for town in the middle of the night. My Grandpa stopped the wagon at the porch, but told me not to get out yet. He got out and came around to my side and offered me his hand. "You thought I didn't know how to treat a lady, didn't you?" he said with a grin.

I laughed and gave him my hand and acted as elegant as a body could be while sitting behind a sway-back mule. The preacher and his wife came out on the porch and smiled broadly as I stepped down. My Grandpa bowed and got back up in the wagon. He called back as he turned the mule toward home, "I'm proud of you, Grace." Though he had a smile, I saw a little bit of fear in his face, and what I believed to be a tear. I wonder if he was afraid I wouldn't come back to him, or that I would come back so changed that he wouldn't know me.

We ate a small supper and then the preacher's wife said that it was time to go to bed. I could hardly sleep, thinking about all the excitement to come. The next thing I knew, though, the preacher's wife was gently saying that it was time to get ready. At first, I was going to beg for more sleep, but then I remembered where I was, and the adventure before us and I sprang out of the bed quicker than Stonewall Jackson pouncing on a mouse. I dressed so quickly that I was quite rumpled, but I did not have to worry. The preacher's wife was there to straighten it all out.

I'd seen the train many times, of course, but I had never ridden on it. During the war, there was never much encouragement from the Yankees to ride the train, since they were afraid of spies and all. Also, there was the danger that the Confederates would derail the train. They didn't care who was on it if they were in the mood to kill some Yankees. Anyway, there was hardly ever any room because so many soldiers had to be moved back and forth. Plus, we never had the money or any reason to go anywhere.

Now we did. The preacher's wife took care of the money part and let me sit by the window. I watched farms that took many steps to cross, disappear in a hurry. I'd see a building coming up and then it would be behind us. I couldn't believe the world rushing by outside the train. The preacher's wife was delighted at how thrilled I was at the sights. I could hardly eat the lunch she packed for us, but she encouraged me so kindly that I had to try.

After many stops to let people on and off, we arrived at the edge of Nashville. I thought I had seen buildings and lots of people before, but I realized I had not. They had buildings taller than the biggest barn I had ever seen. They had so many Union soldiers, I wondered if the war was truly over. The train station came into view and it was packed tighter than a bunch of flabby politicians at a free pig roast.

I didn't feel tired at all, even though we'd been traveling for most of the day. We got off the train and, almost immediately, an old Negro man popped up.

"Miss Caroline, it is so good to see you," he almost yelled.

"Rufus, it's good to see you, too," the preacher's wife returned.

He looked down at me. "And this must be Miss Grace."

I curtsied and said, "Pleased to meet you, Rufus."

He tossed his head back and laughed heartily. "Miss Caroline, I know who's been teaching her. Yes, I do." He looked up and down the train and said, "I'll get your bags, ma'am. The carriage is on the street in front."

The preacher's wife said, "We'll wait for you there."

We made our way through the herd of people, and the preacher's wife found the carriage. It was beautiful, with every piece of wood shined real bright, and the horses wore fancy harnesses.

While we waited, I asked the preacher's wife about Rufus. "Is he a slave?" I whispered.

"He was. Now he works for us."

"Was he your slave?" I wondered.

"He was my father's slave. He took care of him from the time he was a young boy."

So the preacher's wife came from a family of slave owners. Nothing she had ever said or done had ever given up that fact. I stopped asking questions, and Rufus joined us in no time, flung our bags on the back like they weighed nothing at all, and we were off down the grand street in our queenly carriage. I couldn't believe how lucky I was to be carried about in something so grand.

As we rode along, the state capitol building came into view and it was so big I could hardly speak. We rode a block or two more, and stopped in front of this most beautiful mansion. I looked back and was pleased that I could still see the capitol. I was surprised when Rufus started announcing our arrival. "Git up now," he yelled to no one I could see. "Miss Caroline and Miss Grace are home."

Suddenly, a Negro boy came out to steady the horses for us while Rufus helped us from the carriage. We walked up the steps of the grand house, and when we almost reached the front door, it opened, and this very tall gentleman emerged. He still carried some documents in his hands and funny glasses on his nose. He reached toward the preacher's wife, gave her a small hug and said, "Dear Caroline. Welcome home," he added firmly and formally.

"Father, this is Grace," and I had to curtsey once again.

"Pleased to meet you, Mr. Harris," I said what I had rehearsed so many times.

"Grace Meadows, it is an honor," he said back to me gallantly.

He told us to come in, and suggested to his daughter that we go to our rooms and freshen up from our trip.

Our rooms! I couldn't believe that we didn't have to share.

The preacher's wife took me to my room and showed me where everything was. Someone had already brought in fresh water in the pitcher, and I scrubbed my face and looked myself over in the mirror. She had told me to lie down for a few minutes and she'd be back for me, but I was too excited to do that. I ran around the room, looking at everything and peering at the sights from the window. I guess the preacher's wife heard me galloping around the room because she came back shortly and invited me to her room. I accepted and was astonished to see that her room was fancier than the one I had been in. There were lace and ruffles and gorgeous dark wood and a shiny chandelier.

I asked the preacher's wife how she could leave all this for a cabin in the woods and she smiled. "Love can take you to the strangest places," she revealed.

There was a knock on the door and when the preacher's wife asked who it was, we learned it was her mother. The preacher's wife arose and met her mother, and they embraced warmly. "My dear, did you have a good journey?"

"Yes, Mother."

"Good. I am glad. Your father is eager for you to come down. He's so excited about his plans for education of the Negroes." The lady looked down at me. "Grace, you are so welcome here. Caroline has written of you often."

I blushed to think that the woman I had admired so, had told so many people about me. I stared at her and forgot my manners. I didn't curtsey or say, "Pleased to meet you" or anything. The preacher's wife gave a small laugh and said, "I think she's overwhelmed."

"I can see that," her mother said, smiling slightly.

After her mother left, I was so embarrassed that I hadn't said anything. "Don't worry, Grace. You'll have plenty of time to talk to her. Maybe you should lie down just for a minute."

I told her there was no way I could sleep, but she asked me to try. I closed my eyes, and the next thing I knew, she was waking me to get ready for supper.

I got brushed and fluffed, and walked with her down the tall staircase. I could hear that it wouldn't be a small family gathering. I heard several men's voices booming, and the lilt of women's voices. I got very nervous, thinking that my first meal that would test my manners would be in such a big crowd.

The preacher's wife was swept up immediately in "Caroline Carson, how-wonderful-to-see-yous" and "Caroline, you-are-looking-lovelys." She had trouble keeping track of me, even though I wasn't the one moving around.

After a lot of what the preacher's wife had said beforehand would be "small talk," supper was served. The preacher's wife made sure that I was seated beside her. I didn't have to decide how much to take of each dish because a Negro woman came around and served everyone silently. There was laughter and lots of food and wine. I wondered if the preacher knew that his wife and her family took a drink or two.

A few people spoke to me, but I didn't have to worry about what to say because mostly the conversation was about how to rebuild. After we were full as ticks, we moved to the other room, and they started to talk of the main reason for their gathering. The Negro question. How to educate them and put them to work. They talked long and argued hard. They divided Middle Tennessee into different sections, and decided who would be in charge of each part. What puzzled me was that the entire time they talked, they did not bother to ask the opinion of the Negroes who moved in and out of the room in silent service.

When I made the preacher's wife aware of that fact, she was silent for a moment, then said, "That's a good point, Grace. I'll remedy that before we leave." I don't believe that she did it the next day or the day after that, because we spent so much time visiting and seeing the sights of the city. They have lanterns on the street that burn something called gas! One market near the railroad that was frequented by the Yankee soldiers, their wives and certain select Southerners, had more food in it than I had seen in all the summers of my life. I asked the preacher's wife why her family got to shop there, and she made the surprising announcement, "My father was a Unionist."

"What?" I exclaimed. "How can he be a Unionist when he owned slaves?"

She thought for a moment and then explained, "He's comfortable with his contradictions." I decided that it was easier to be a Unionist in a big city held by the Yankee soldiers and fortified against attack. Her father wouldn't have had the Confederates poking at him every night, telling him he was wrong in his beliefs. A Unionist slave owner in my part of the woods wouldn't have survived the war.

Everywhere we went, we were met with hustle and pockets of abundance. There were streets we did not go down, and when I asked about it, I was told politely that nice ladies did not go there. I peered down one of those streets and saw a big man dragging his wife. He was yelling for her to get his supper, and not one person, even the Union soldiers with guns, did anything to help her.

I didn't understand what I had seen, and asked the preacher's wife about it. At first, she was alarmed that I had seen such a sight. Then she listened gravely as I said, "I thought the war was fought to end slavery."

"There are different views, Grace, but yes, that is one of them."

"Yet, that woman is that man's slave."

"Yes, I guess that she is."

I realized then that there are different types of slavery. I wondered if there would ever be a war to end the kind I had seen that day.

***

Mr. Harris had a huge room that he used as a library. I could tell that he loved his books, and had spent quite a bit of time learning about the war. It looked like he had collected everything ever written about the war. He offered to let me explore his library if I promised to be very, very careful.

I eagerly promised I would be. I looked at his books first. He had *Uncle Tom's Cabin*, the book Mr. Lincoln said had started all this trouble. Mr. Harris had all kinds of speeches that the abolitionists had given. He showed me his newspapers he had kept, going back over twenty years. I marveled at what I saw. As I read, I could see the war coming. They thought big compromises would help. Anyone could have seen that they would not, not with tempers so hot.

I also was shocked by the advertisements. Of course, by now I knew that slaves had been bought and sold like livestock, but I had never seen it in print: "Negro girl for sale. I will sell to the highest bidder a Negro girl who is about six years of age."

I was silent at supper, and Mrs. Harris asked if something was wrong. "Yes ma'am. I'm worried about the Negro girl I saw for sale."

She looked surprised. "What do you mean, dear? Who is selling a Negro girl?"

"Someone in the paper."

Mr. Harris explained that I had been looking over old papers, and she understood. "That's all over now. No need to worry anymore," she assured me.

I kept picking at my food, then asked, "Did the two of you ever sell a child?"

They looked at each other ashamedly, and I knew that no matter what they said, the answer was "yes." I looked around the fancy room and was glad that I lived on a little farm in a corner of Sumner County, far from the stench of slavery.

That night, the preacher's wife tried to explain. "Sometimes it takes a long time to realize that some things are wrong. My parents were born to wealth. They grew up with slaves. Their parents inherited slaves. It's not so easy to say that your parents, grandparents and everyone up the ancestral line was wrong."

"What is so hard about realizing that a six-year-old girl should stay with her parents?"

The preacher's wife opened her mouth, but nothing came out. She finished brushing my hair and then said, "I guess you'll have to give me more time to give you a good answer to that. All I can say is that my parents are trying. Try to give them some credit for that."

The days passed quickly, and so much was packed into them that I hardly had time to even make it into the kitchen. When I did, I came upon Rufus, his wife, Rosella and their daughter, Alice. They seemed surprised to see me, then glad. Rosella gave me a piece of pie and a glass of milk. I asked Rufus what was the difference between being a slave and being a servant.

He looked surprised at my interest, but he thought on the question and said, "Well, you get money. I guess the answer is, though, that you get a choice."

"A choice of what?"

"Whether you work for nothing and have no gratitude, or work for just a little bit and have to say thanks." He gave a big laugh and Rosella added a chuckle.

Once he stopped laughing, he added, "I guess the real choice is that you can go or you can stay."

I nodded my head because I thought I understood. Then I asked, "Why don't you go?"

"Miss Grace, you ask the hard questions," he said laughing. "Where would an old man like me go?" I think he was laughing at the thought that he really had a choice.

I asked Rufus and Rosella if they knew anything about Mr. Harris selling a little Negro child. They shut their mouths real tight and wouldn't say another word. They left to get to their chores, while Alice stayed in the kitchen. Alice came over to me real close and said, "I know."

"What? Tell me, please," I pleaded.

She went back to washing the dishes, and I thought she wouldn't tell me unless I really begged, and so I did. Finally, when she knew I was down to my last beg, she told me.

"Mr. Harris has a big farm down in Maury County. He probably had fifty slaves down there. Well, one day one of the women turned up with child. Well, that's nothing new, but the baby came out light-skinned. Well, everyone just figured the overseer was the father, or maybe some visitor to the farm took some liberties. Then the word came that Mr. and Mrs. Harris were coming to visit the farm. Well, mother and child were swept up so fast, you'd think they'd been eaten by locusts. After the Harrises left, the mother comes back with nothing but her tears. So everyone figured that child's father was Mr. Harris, and she had to go."

I didn't say anything, because I was feeling too shocked to react. Alice added, "That's what I know. It's the truth."

I kept munching on my pie and looking at Alice. I decided it was best to speak of other things until I decided how I felt about it. "I can do my multiplication tables up to twelve times twelve," I boasted.

She didn't say anything.

"I can spell words that have ten letters in them."

She still didn't say anything.

"Tell me about something you've read."

Then she told me something else that shocked me: "I can't read."

That was one of the most surprising things I learned in Nashville. "How old are you?"

"Ten."

"Ten years old. You should be able to read plenty."

"I can't."

"Why not?"

"My Daddy can't read. My Mama don't read." Then she added with a hint of contempt, "Nobody ever taught me."

That evening, when the group of teachers-to-be came to discuss the plans for the education of the Negroes, I stayed silent until I could stand it no more. "Mr. Harris, did you know that Alice can't read?"

"Who is Alice?" asked one of the guests.

"The girl who works in Mr. Harris's kitchen," I said. As soon as it was out of my mouth, I knew I had done the wrong thing. Mr. Harris turned beet-red. Mrs. Harris's jaw dropped. The preacher's wife, the woman I always wanted to please, looked shocked.

None of the guests said a word until someone said, "Mrs. Harris, the sweet potatoes were delightful. You must give me the recipe."

The preacher's wife was always gentle with my spirit, so she only gently chastised me that night.

"Grace, perhaps you need to learn that the truth doesn't always need to be spoken so directly." She smiled a little. "Or maybe it doesn't need to be spoken so directly in front of so many people."

The next morning, no one woke me for breakfast. I guess I had gotten used to big city ways and was sleeping as late as 7:00. As I made my way down the stairs, I could hear Mr. Harris talking. "You and Thomas need to come back to Nashville. What is there for you out there in the middle of nowhere?"

I was proud of the preacher's wife as she defended, "Father, it's not 'nowhere' to me. We do important work there."

"You can do so much here. We get so worried about you out there," Mrs. Harris pleaded.

"If we survived the war, I believe we can survive Reconstruction," the preacher's wife declared.

"How bad is it out there?" Mr. Harris asked sympathetically.

"It's a little better now. There's still no money to speak of, but at least people aren't losing what little they grow or gather to the soldiers or marauders. The people are strong. Most of them still have unbroken spirits."

"The Scots-Irish will never be broken, my dear," said Mrs. Harris haughtily.

"Speaking of broken spirits, how is Grace's father? Has there been any word?"

"No, Father. I do not know how that will turn out. Poor Grace has been through so much. I fear for her if her father does not return."

Mr. Harris chuckled in such a way that I knew that he had forgiven me for my announcement the previous night. "I fear not for Grace. We need to fear *her*."

As the preacher's wife and I rode the train home the next day, I thought over the events and lessons of the past weeks. Some sights had awed me. Some revelations had pained me. I couldn't decide if I was glad I had gone to Nashville. Was it better to have something to look forward to? Was it better to think that everything was pretty in a city far away?

As I thought about it all, it hit me that if the war had not happened, the preacher's wife would have inherited the farm with all the slaves, including Rufus, Rosella and Alice. I asked her what she would have done with the slaves.

"That's easy. Thomas said he wouldn't marry me unless I promised to free them. So that decision wasn't going to require any deep thinking."

I was very proud of my preacher then. But then I wondered to her what she would have done if the preacher hadn't insisted she promise.

"Grace, I'd like to say that I would have freed them. But I'll be honest. I haven't had to make that decision. The slaves were worth a lot of money. The farm is worth nothing without them. In fact, my father had to sell the farm because he couldn't afford to pay wages and still make money."

I asked, "What happened to the slaves? Oh, I guess I should say the people who used to be slaves."

"Some had already left. A few remained. Some of them are working on the farm for the new owner, but he didn't need them all. We tried to find work for the rest on other farms. Those remaining were given some corn meal and $1.00 and sent on their way."

I have to say that I was somewhat disappointed that the preacher's wife didn't know for sure whether she would be a slave owner or not. I guess she's right though. You don't know if you'd give away wealth unless you've got it to give.

I wondered if the preacher's wife knew about the slave child that Mr. Harris had fathered. The child would be her little sister. I was dying to ask her, but I knew I had better not. It might get Alice in trouble, for one thing. And I knew that it would give my dear teacher pain. So I kept my questions within.

The train kept moving us toward our homes, and I became sad when I remembered that my Daddy would not be there for me. I couldn't help but feel some bitterness that my Daddy was still in turmoil from fighting a war to keep the Harrises in their finery. I thought of Mr. Harris and his contradictions, and feared the contradictions to come in my own life. If Mr. Harris could not see his that glared so harshly, I wondered if there was any hope for me.

I thought about my trip to Nashville for some time, but I never thought of the city in the same way. Still, I decided that I was glad that I went, especially when I got a letter from Alice. She didn't write the whole letter, which said that she was learning to read. I was right proud, though, when I saw that she had signed her name herself.

15

For five months we waited to get more news of my Daddy. While we waited for Daddy or a letter about him, Grandma and Grandpa talked even less than usual. I'd catch them looking off down the road at all times of the day. I did, too. We were looking for Daddy or some good news. I wonder if Grandma was praying she wouldn't receive the bad news she had dreaded for so long. Nobody admitted that we were worrying about Daddy, but we were.

One day, in the middle of a bright, windy afternoon, we heard the dogs yapping like the Yankees had finally come to carry us all away, and we all rushed to the front porch to see what was coming toward us. Surely, it wasn't Daddy, because the dogs wouldn't carry on like that. But it was. He wasn't alone, though. He had a woman and a little girl with him. She looked to be about three years old. I guess the dogs had been barking at the strangers. I hated to think that Daddy had been gone so long that the dogs didn't even know him.

Daddy helped the woman and child down from the wagon. "Where'd you get the wagon, Daddy?" I asked.

He said it was my new Mama's wagon. I eyed the woman who made no effort to smile or look at me. I was disappointed because I think my real Mama would have. This woman looked over the cabin slowly, never saying a word to anybody. Her face was grim and tight. Her brown hair was pulled back so far that I thought her dark eyes would pop out of her head. The little girl, Katie, looked at me with great hope. She smiled and I smiled back. She looked away shyly.

"I don't need a new Mama, Daddy. Grandma is doing fine as a Mama."

"Hush, girl," said my Grandma, even though she looked pleased. She looked back at the woman and told her, "Welcome." The woman nodded her head.

"Where'd you find them, Daddy?" I wanted to know.

"You got the letter?"

"Yes, Daddy."

"That man I had no cause to kill. This is his family. His parents were trying to care for them, but they couldn't afford it. After they stopped yelling at me and stopped trying to kill me, they told me to take them," he said gesturing at the woman and the girl.

"Did you two marry yet?" Grandma asked.

"No ma'am, but I'm willing if she is."

"Come on in and eat and let's talk about it."

My Grandma put out a big spread and we ate a lot. After we had our fill, the little girl and I went outside to play.

"Your Daddy killed my Daddy," she said.

"He's sorry. Besides, your Daddy was a Yankee."

The little blonde girl didn't have anything to say to that. I guess everyone knew you were supposed to hate Yankees. We walked some more and I showed her the pretty cow and the sway-back mule, and she was impressed. I have to say, though, that their wagon and horse were mighty pretty, too. I was glad they were ours now. I showed her around the farm and found out she sure didn't know much. She didn't know that you can eat pokeberry leaves, which we had to, many a time. She didn't know that the mares' tails in the sky meant it was going to rain tomorrow. I was about to get mad at her when I realized that Little Bess wouldn't have known anything herself. That I'd have to teach her. I guess that's what babies are—someone to teach and give some love to. I got nice again and Katie seemed to like me. I decided to like her, too, and wondered if you were supposed to hate little Yankee girls. I'd have to ask Grandma. I decided that Katie wouldn't be too much trouble. After all, I didn't take up the whole bed, and it might be nice to have someone to talk to. Someone who wasn't so worried about chores and what was coming around the bend at them.

She ran back to the cabin because she was missing her Mama. I wished I had my own Mama to run home to, but I had to be a big girl and accept that I never would. I didn't know about that woman as my Mama. I had to think about that.

After Katie left, I went and sat by the creek. Grandma and Daddy didn't see me sitting there when they walked by. I heard Grandma say that we could hardly feed what we got now. "How we gonna feed two more?"

"It's something I got to do, even if I have to go somewhere else."

"There's no cause for you to leave, son. Not again. I just wanted you to think about it." Grandma stooped and picked an Indian pink that was fading. "It won't be long before we'll have to get the crop in."

"We'll both help. I've seen Susan work. She'll be able to do a lot. I'll do more, I promise. I've been in that war, still. I'm going to try to let it go. I've done all I could do to make it better."

"Do you love her, son?"

"Does that matter now?"

"I don't know. I wish that I did," Grandma lamented.

"Mother, I think that any love I deserved lies up on that hill. Now I'll have to make do with getting these kids grown."

Grandma sent me for the preacher, and Susan and Daddy were married that very day. I hadn't seen but one other wedding, but I have to say that those were the most somber "I do's" I ever hope to hear. Even the ring of daisies I made for Katie's hair didn't seem to help. I guess they were make-do I do's. The ones you do when the one you really want is gone.

Daddy and Susan didn't go anywhere but to *work* for their honeymoon and we began life with these new people. Daddy was right. Susan was a hard worker. She helped Grandma in the kitchen and Daddy in the field. We all thought that war was behind us, and good riddance, I'd say. Daddy never spoke of the battles even when other men came by and wanted to talk about it. "Where'd you fight?" a one-armed man would ask. "How many did you kill?" a blind one would wonder. Remnants of men came by with their questions, but Daddy would always say he didn't remember. Sometimes saying nothing says it all.

The other men told their tales, though. I'd be excited by their stories of thunderous battles and Rebel yells if I didn't know that the end result of it was that Daddy was not the man he was meant to be, and little girls like Katie would never know their fathers. I wonder if half of what they said was true. Those men dodged more bullets, were congratulated by more generals, and rescued more of their fellow soldiers than I ever thought possible in one lifetime.

We got fewer visitors when it was time for the harvest. Maybe having lost an arm or an eye would give a man an audience for his stories, or admiration from the boys, but a missing body part or having a downed spirit was no excuse for not helping bring in the crops. Grandpa and Daddy cut the tobacco, and Susan, Grandma and I walked behind them and spiked it. Even little Katie helped by putting all the leaves that got left behind into one pile. Every little bit helped. We gathered ears of corn, picked beans, squash, tomatoes and cucumbers. We dug the potatoes and pulled up the carrots. Anything that could be eaten now or someday, we kept. Most of the work was done in silence. Sometimes, though, Grandma would break into a tune. Usually, if we knew the song, everyone except Susan would join her. Sometimes it was a hymn and sometimes it was a Stephen Foster tune. My favorite was "Hard Times Come Again No More." I guess when he wrote it, people could only guess what hard times were. After the war, even little children knew.

At noon, Grandma and I went back to the house to get dinner ready, while Susan and Katie and the men kept on working in the fields. As soon as we had a decent meal put together, everyone would come in and eat quickly, for there was no time to dally now. I was old enough and had seen enough hunger to know what the harvest meant. No harvest or a bad harvest meant that the winter would be long and sad and a time of worry as the older folks figured out a way to keep us fed. So I knew it was important to work hard and not complain even if my muscles ached and my fingers bled.

Of course, once everything was picked, cut or dug up, the work was still not over. The tobacco had to be hung to cure high in the barn, and the vegetables needed to be canned. In the field, I thought my legs and arms would fall off. When it was time for the canning, I thought my fingers had seen the end of their days. Still, no matter how much pain we felt, we had to go on.

Even though we worked hard, Daddy seemed to feel better. I wouldn't say he had a spring in his step by any means, but I think he felt a purpose that he hadn't known since he'd come home from the war. That made me feel better.

Despite working side by side with Susan, I didn't know what to think of her. She kept so quiet. We were all thinking that maybe she'd forgotten about that old war. I figured that would be hard for her, but I thought she would just have to if she wanted to go on like everyone else was doing. She'd tend to little Katie, but I didn't see her give much affection to her. I wondered if that was the way she'd always been, or if she had just lost too much during the war. Katie didn't seem to notice, though. She'd just run from person to person, asking for hugs and, of course, she got them, along with a little smile, too. She was a good little girl and she was learning a lot about the farm, although I have to say that she still didn't know nearly as much as I did.

Sometimes I'd lie awake and listen to Katie breathe, and wish that I was as young as she was. You see, if I was that young, I wouldn't know anything about the war and what it had done. I could just look for love like she did, rather than wonder about all the hate that had come before. I wonder if little Bess would have been young enough to escape it just like Katie. As I counted the years, and thought back about what I knew at what age, I figured that even little Bess would have known how bad the war had been. That made me a little sad.

Susan's face never lost that grimness that she had when I first saw her. I tried to make her laugh, but I couldn't even get a smile out of her. Finally, I gave up, figuring she had no room in her heart to love me. I didn't blame her, though. I just hoped that she had known some laughter, back when she had the man she really wanted. Back when she had the hope that he'd come home from the war.

Once the weather was cooler and the canning was done, we had a little time to breathe and take more pleasure in life. There was time to watch and laugh as Stonewall Jackson swatted a corn cob around the porch, and General Beauregard nipped at the heels of Nathan Bedford Forrest, just to make him squeal. I'd hold Katie on the back of Nathan Bedford Forrest, and he'd charge around the barnyard just like the real general was known to do. We'd bundle ourselves up and sit on the porch and listen to a neighbor's fiddle play a mournful tune, and then dance when it quickly changed to a mountain jig. We'd laugh so much and feel so happy that I thought maybe, just maybe, that war would be put to rest. I wondered if this was what it was like before the war. Work, yet good times. Sweat, but laughter. I looked over at Susan and Katie who were just shadows, really. For a moment I imagined that they were my Mama and little Bess joining my Daddy and grandparents on the porch. This is what it could have been like if Bess and my Mama had lived, and Daddy had never gone away.

I realized then how important the porch was to us. It was where many important events had happened. It was where we learned what happened to my Mama. It was where I'd first seen Katie. It was where I first recalled seeing my Daddy in the flesh and not just in some picture.

The days passed, and even though Susan still looked drawn and did not bless us with her laughter or even a smile, we thought that someday she was going to join us in this new life. We just didn't know when. We didn't understand that one man could not be exchanged for another.

One day, Daddy said he was fixin' to walk high up on the ridge to look at the timber. He wanted to decide where we should cut the wood we needed for the winter. He asked me to go along with him.

I was so pleased that he asked me. He walked fast, not slowed down at all by the ax he was carrying, but by now, General Beauregard and I were used to the fast pace of the menfolk. We made it to a beautiful spot where we could look out over the valley and the hills far below, and we sat down to eat a few bites of the cornbread Grandma had sent with us.

This was about the first time we had been alone since I had returned from Nashville. I still had some things on my mind, and I hoped Daddy could help me with them. First, I wondered what he thought the war had been about.

"Grace, do you have to think so deeply on such a beautiful day?"

I thought a moment before I answered, "Yes, I think I do."

He didn't say anything. "Grace, sometimes there are some things a child can't understand." He brushed away a wasp that was exploring his shirt. "Sometimes, there are things that no one can understand. I think that's what you'll have to accept about the war."

I told him that I wasn't sure that would be enough for me. "That war hurt so many people, so many children, that I just don't understand it."

Daddy nodded his head. I continued. "Daddy, there are some people who are saying that the war was all about slavery. Is that what you think?"

He didn't answer.

"Daddy, when I was in Nashville, I met a ten-year-old Negro girl who couldn't read. Is that why you fought the war? So that little girl would never learn to read? I heard about another little Negro girl being taken from her mama and sold for money. Is that why you fought the war? So that little girl could be sold?"

As I asked the question, I prayed that he would have another explanation for me for why we fought the war. But he did not.

I have seen shame. I have felt shame. But I don't think that I will ever see again the kind of shame I saw on my father's face that day. I hope that I will never feel again the shame I felt, because I was the one who had given it to him.

He didn't say anything. He picked up his ax and started walking along the ridge. I didn't know whether to follow. He did not look back or call for me, so I sat and patted General Beauregard until Daddy was out of sight. I decided that I would never ask my Daddy about the war again. I went back to the cabin without him.

He avoided me as much as possible during the next few days. I guess he was running from the pointy questions my Grandma tells me I ask too many of. I wondered if he would ever ask me to walk with him again, and I regretted having my curious nature, because it had driven a wedge between my father and me. When I had almost given up hope of knowing my Daddy, and understanding why he did what he did, he came to me in the cornfield. He said he was going up on the ridge to cut some timber and wanted to know if I would go with him. I said I sure would, and grinned, and so did he.

He already had the sway-back mule hitched up to the skidder and he lifted me and settled me into the back of the mule. Daddy led us back to the place where I had asked too many questions, the ridge I will always think of as the ridge of shame, and he took me from the mule, and we sat down together.

"I thought I was doing the right thing, Grace. Most of the young men here were joining the Confederacy. The Union soldiers were gathering to invade us. I thought I was protecting my family. I didn't stop to think about what it was really about." He stopped and gazed down into the valley. "If I knew then what I know now, I would have packed up this whole family and moved west. At that time, that never occurred to me."

I was watching him, fascinated. I don't think my Daddy had ever spoken so many words to anyone all at once.

He continued. "Your Mama didn't want me to go, but she respected my decision. I think she knew that I would feel shame if I hadn't gone." He stood up and faced me. "Grace, you also need to understand that we didn't think it would last that long. Or be that hard. We didn't expect that our land would be ruined. Our families killed. We didn't think about slavery. The men I fought with, the men I was in prison with, we didn't talk about slaves. We didn't have slaves before we joined. We knew we wouldn't have them after the war. For us, the war wasn't about why. It was about trying to survive one more day."

He turned from me and looked back to the valley. "Grace, I sure didn't expect to lose your Mama. I know that I've let you down. But as you examine the world, try to remember not to be too harsh to those who didn't even know they were being tested."

It meant a lot to him when I said, "All right, Daddy."

He added, "Try to forgive those who have a hard time forgiving themselves."

I comforted him by saying, "I will try, Daddy." But I wasn't sure I could, as long as Bertram Manning lived. As long as I didn't understand why my father left my Mama and me.

16

Once it started getting cold, I started going to learn with the preacher's wife again. When it was planting time, or harvest time or canning time, I just couldn't go. Once we were ready for winter, though, Grandma would tell me it was time for my studies. "Maybe you won't have a life as hard as we have had if you know how to read," she said.

So many girls, or boys, for that matter, didn't know how to read. Their folks didn't see the importance of it, I guess. On a farm, you have to read the signs of the forest and of the winds, of the meadows and the skies, but little squiggles on a page, what has that to do with farming? Maybe I should be thankful to that mean man for trying to cheat my Grandpa. Maybe that's why they thought it was so important for me to learn more.

Katie would go with me to see the preacher's wife. Not that she learned much. I tried to teach her a few letters, but she didn't see the sense of it, I guess. Still, she liked to tag along, and she would amuse herself with some dolls that the preacher's wife had, or she'd draw pictures in the dust or simply watch us as we learned our lessons.

One day after the other children had left, and Katie and I were fixin' to leave, the preacher's wife stopped us. "How is Susan getting on at your farm?" she asked.

"I'm not sure, ma'am," I answered. "She's very quiet and nothing anyone says or does can make a smile come out."

The preacher's wife looked grave. "I've noticed that myself. She doesn't seem to want to visit, or join in any of our groups."

"We've been very busy, as you know," I reminded her. The preacher and his wife had a small farm, but they didn't depend as much on the land as we did.

The preacher's wife gave me a small smile and said, "That's true, I suppose." That's one of the things I liked most about her. You didn't have to search too far for a bit of joy in her.

I was still most curious about the preacher's wife. Like how she met the preacher. When I asked her, she got a faraway look and said that her family always made it a point to invite promising young men from the seminary to dinner.

"How many young men did you entertain?" I wondered.

"Oh, I couldn't count them. My father knew that they were lonely, being away from home. And the food at the seminary couldn't compare to Rosella's cooking. I don't think anyone ever turned us down."

"Did you and the preacher fall in love right from the start?"

She laughed. "Well, I think he did. He had to work on me a bit."

"Why was that?" I asked.

"You see, preachers don't make very much money. My parents were afraid that he couldn't support me. Or that he wanted me for our money."

"How long did it take you to decide that you loved him?"

She looked at me with amused eyes. "Grace, you still are direct, aren't you?"

"Is that so bad?"

She reached over and gently rubbed my head. "No, honey. I guess it saves time."

I noticed that she still hadn't answered my question. "Well, how long?"

"Let's see. You know, it's strange. I've thought so little about my life before coming here. Before the war. It seems to have wiped out all memory." She went over and sat down on the porch and started rocking. She looked over at Katie who was chasing a puppy who whirled and twirled so swiftly that it would not be caught. When it decided to turn from the pursued into the pursuer, it turned on Katie who giggled with delight as she ran from it.

"I guess it was about six weeks," she continued.

"Is that quick?"

She laughed a bit. "For my family it sure was. For me, too, I guess. I knew that he had all the qualities I admired. If he had been a wealthy man, my family would have been thrilled. So I decided that the money didn't matter, where we lived didn't matter, that I could say goodbye to the parties and the elegance." She looked down the road as she added, "It was the right decision in more ways than one. You see, the wealth, the parties, they would have been gone anyway. The war ended all that."

"How old were you when you married?"

"Nineteen."

"Lots of girls around here get married younger than that."

She looked at me and said, "That's true. That may change, though. There are fewer men now."

I started down the steps, but I turned back to her because I figured she knew as much about love as anyone. "If you love someone, I mean really love them, can you ever really love another person?"

She thought over my question a moment. "I've never been through that myself. Oh, I had infatuations, that's for sure. But once I fell in love, I mean really fell in love, well, you just know that it's different from infatuation. I don't know whether it ever comes again."

"So if you lost the preacher, do you think you'd never marry again?"

"I can't say. I know that it would be lonely. But I can't imagine being with anyone else for a long time."

I turned and got to the bottom step and then turned back to her. "Do you think my Daddy can ever love Susan the way he loved my Mama?"

"I sure hope so, honey. I think he wants to."

"Do you think Susan wants to love him?"

She considered her answer carefully. "I think Susan is too worn down to do it now. But maybe someday she'll realize there's good in him. Probably that day won't come until *he* realizes that he's still worthy of love."

I called for Katie who skipped over to me. I waved goodbye to the preacher's wife as I called back to her. "Thank you, ma'am."

17

I thought a lot about what the preacher's wife said about my Daddy needing to feel worthy of love. I did my best to make him feel his worth, and said many a prayer that he would. I even talked to the men who had fought in the war, in order to try to understand better. At first they thought I wanted to hear about battles and killing, but I told them no, I wanted to understand what the battles do to the ones who survive, not how a cunning general had managed to outwit one who was not so clever at that particular moment. When I convinced those men that I wanted to know how the war affected them, they'd look mighty somber and look around to make sure that no one was listening except me. They'd steal a nip from the bottle they carried and say, "Honey, it was awful. Just awful." Then they usually started to cry, and they would slowly start up the road and wouldn't return for some time. I guess they were embarrassed that a little girl knew how they really felt about the war. That it wasn't about banners and bugles, but about being frightened, bewildered, cold and alone. Even though you were surrounded by thousands of men. Even though it might be summer and the cannons added even more scorching heat to the air. I learned that the worst thing they felt at that moment, though, was not feeling worthy of love.

That was the feeling that continued for these men. This is a small community and it's hard to keep any secrets, so when I heard tales of wives with bruises, of men blind with drink, and children who feared their fathers, I knew that it would be a long time, if ever, before these men would feel worthy of love again.

Daddy was good to us, and so we were luckier than most. Still, I would look at him and Susan at the breakfast table and wonder what it would have been like to look up and see my Daddy and Mama looking at each other with love and longing. I think my Daddy was searching for his way back to love, and when I saw him swing Katie onto his shoulders, or when he asked me to join him on a walk to the high fields where he would hold my hand as we went, I thought he had found it.

I enjoyed these walks with my Daddy and I even got brave enough to ask what it was like in the prison camp. "I thought the battlefield was horrible," he said with a faraway look. "I thought it showed what a man was made of." He walked farther and added, "I was wrong."

I waited for him to add more, but he didn't for many minutes. Finally, he continued, "We nearly starved. Once I ate a rat and was glad to have it. The water—filthy. A little stream of water ran through our…," he hesitated. "I can't call them quarters—it was too awful to be called that. I'll say, 'pen.'

Yes, it was a pen—a pen for gallant young men." He laughed grimly. "The stream—sometimes it wasn't too foul. That saved some of us, too." After another long pause, he told me, "Probably killed others."

Though I could tell he was weary, I asked him to go on. "We had to fight for everything. Food, a cup, blankets, boots. You'd go to sleep owning all that, and wake up and it'd all be gone. Gangs of men would steal from those weakened by illness or lack of food. If they grew tired of stealing, they'd kill weaker men in front of everyone."

"Were you a part of those gangs, Daddy?"

He answered after a moment. "Some Tennessee men and I formed a group for protection only. We took back what was taken from us. That was a bad fight. We got everything back, though," he said with no emotion.

Once he got started, he didn't seem to want to stop talking about it. "It was hard to stay on top. You'd have a strong group, then some of the best fighters would die or be too sick to be of any use. Some new prisoners would be brought in and they'd join the other group. Those were long days." He paused, then added, "Of all the things I did during the war, I'm most ashamed of what I became in that prison."

He only spoke of those days when he was with me. He never spoke of the Yankee prison in front of Grandpa and Grandma. With them, he only spoke of the farm and raising children.

I know that Grandma and Grandpa felt better that he was home and seemed settled. They tried to reach out to Susan who did not respond. They did not seem to hold anything against her, for they knew that she, too, was trying to find her new place in this world.

Susan would go for many walks by herself, sometimes disappearing without a word. She'd reappear in silence and resume her chores at a steady pace. No one, not even Katie, questioned where she had been. Once, I followed her, and I watched as she sat high on the river's bluff, not moving. I did not see any evidence that these walks or the contemplation gave her peace, for she continued to look more drawn into herself.

According to the news I overheard from the preacher or the guests who came to our door, the whole South was having a terrible time of it. There still was no money, and there were taxes to pay and seed to buy. There were men with no farms or there were farms with no men. We still had to dance around the Yankees who demanded so much from people with so little. Crushed spirits. We seemed to have plenty of those. People who trudged on. That, we could offer. That is all we had to give. I just hoped that was enough. I guess it would have to be.

One day when I was particularly worried, I talked to the preacher about it. "Brother Carson, will we make it?" I asked him.

"Don't worry, honey. God will provide."

"Will he, Preacher? Will God do that?"

I think the preacher could see then that a simple answer would not do for me. He knelt down to me, took my hand

and said, "Yes, Grace. As long as there are children like you to help him."

As I thought about it that night after everyone had settled down to sleep, I hated to think that the whole survival of the South depended upon me. Even though I worked hard and tried to do good, I did not see how I could be such a help to God. I've heard the preacher talk of God's will. If God the Almighty had a will, what could a little girl like me do about it? Was it God's will for the world to be handed to children when the older folks had ruined it and given up hope?

When I asked the preacher that question, he smiled at me and said, "I'll have to study some more, Grace, to keep ahead of you."

When I looked puzzled, he said, "I'm the preacher, but that doesn't mean I know everything. All I know, honey, is that we have to pray. We have to try to 'do justly.' We have to love mercy and walk humbly with God."

18

I looked up the verse that the preacher quoted, and found that the prophet Micah had given it to us. I read it to the family that night. I usually read some verses to them every night before we went to bed. Sometimes my Grandma would tell me what to read. Other times they let me pick the Scripture. I sometimes chose something near where the preacher had preached the Sunday before. Sometimes I let the Bible fall open and I would start from there. This time, though, I chose what the preacher had just told me. Susan rarely made any request or comment except when I read from the Old Testament. She perked right up and asked me to read it three times.

That verse from Micah made me think. What could make you behave justly in these times? We were having a hard time in the South, but even our Tennessee President, Andy

Johnson, couldn't give us any help because the Radical Republicans in Congress kept biting at him. They wanted to punish us for the war, when everyone knows we were minding our own business until the Northern Army came down here. So was that justice, to punish the men like my Daddy who thought they were doing the right thing? Was it justice to make my grandparents suffer when they were only trying to hang on to the farm? And what about me and little Katie who had nothing to do with anything? Where was the mercy? We sure hadn't seen any of it.

During the war, I heard all manner of cussin' against Abe Lincoln, yet after he died you couldn't hear enough nice things about him. The winds sure change. I guess everyone thought he'd be treating us better than we were being treated now. He did seem to have a kind face, one that seemed to know the meaning of forgiveness. I guess everyone's thinking that he would have welcomed us back like the prodigal son. I know that we sure could have used the fatted calf. Or even a skinny one.

I wish Susan had learned the whole verse from Micah. Particularly the part about mercy. She must not have, though. I guess she did what most people do—pick the part from the Bible that suits them, that gives them permission to hate or to divide, the part that thinks justice means the death of the Old Testament instead of the mercy of the New. I wondered if my Daddy felt the same.

We found out that he must have, on the day that we heard a shot out by the river. I ran to find Daddy lying on a bluff, dead, shot through the chest, with Susan standing over him with his revolver in her hands.

"Why'd you kill my Daddy?" I cried.

She looked surprised, and stared at the revolver and my Daddy. She dropped the pistol and fell to her knees. She started to sob with me and said, "He was a good man, but I couldn't forget. It's so odd. He didn't even try to stop me."

She walked toward the river while I cradled my Daddy's head in my arms, not worrying about all the blood running out on the rock and on my clothes. Before she jumped into the river, Susan turned back to me and begged, "Take care of my Katie."

I didn't want to take care of Katie at first. I told her, "Your Mama killed my Daddy." She screamed at me, "Your Daddy killed mine *first*." I called her a filthy pig Yankee. She called me a dirty dog Reb. We both cried, but my heart softened when I realized that some of her tears were for my Daddy. I knew then that she had liked him and that she wanted him to be her Daddy, too.

I decided to take care of her then like I think my Daddy would have. I expect that she will stay with me until the day one of us is carried up that hill. I figure we'll be two orphans trying to understand why we were denied a simple life with our parents.

It is strange to think that if that war had never come and shattered families and regrouped those who remained, then I never would have had a sister. Being with Katie was the only good thing that came to me from that war.

Now I sit near little Bess' grave and look over the fresh mounds of earth that house the earthly remains of Susan,

Daddy and Mama. I have in my hand another letter, this time from someone other than that Bertram Manning. It is from a soldier who was a prisoner with my Daddy. It seems we are always getting letters that bring shock to us. He wrote to thank my Daddy for being good to him, for looking after him when he was an eighteen-year-old boy who didn't know much, under the circumstances. He said that my Daddy noticed that he was down to a cup that leaked, and a ratty blanket. My Daddy took them and played poker with them, brought them back to him along with some boots, an unmarred woolen blanket and an overcoat. He wrote, "I'm sure that saved my life." I was slightly shocked by the news that my father played poker, because gambling was not allowed in our home. What really shocked me was his next statement. "Don't feel bad for taking the oath of allegiance to the Union. How were we to know that the war was finally going to end? I guess that will mean no pension from the state of Tennessee for us, our wives or children, but don't despair. I am confident that a worthy man like you will make it."

I will think of my Daddy often. It won't be like that Mr. Shakespeare says:

> The painful warrior famoused for fight,
> After a thousand victories once foiled,
> Is from the books of honor razed quite,
> And all the rest forgot for which he toiled.

My Daddy gave years and his beloved wife for the Confederacy, and now we find after his death that they will not recognize him as one of theirs. They have forgotten what he gave when they sounded the bugle. But I will not.

The letter from the young Confederate made me wonder if we can ever really know a person. To my grandparents, my Daddy was the son who would always be welcome. To Susan, he was a murderer. To Katie, he was the only father she had known. To this young soldier, he was a hero, yet my father thought himself an animal. To Bertram Manning, he was both the redeemer and the redeemed. My father will always be a wonder to me. I knew pieces of him. Would I ever know the whole man?

Being a daughter, I don't think I will ever fully understand why fathers go to war. Yet, I can be proud of my father. My Daddy tried to do right, but failed. He tried to see right, but did not. He tried to make things right, but could not. Yet, he will always be a hero to me, not because he got dressed up and marched off to war, not because he fired a rifle or waved a bayonet, but because he tried to make things right in the end. That is all any of us can do.

My Daddy had two wives, but short happiness. I know that he had some happiness, because Grandma said that's where little Bess and I came from. In a way I'm glad little Bess is not alone anymore. I had my parents awhile and now she should have them. She should be happier now that both parents are with her, and maybe she can make Susan happy, too. I know my Daddy couldn't, but surely little Bess can.

I've heard that the wages of sin is death. The preacher didn't add that, sometimes, other people pay those wages. I can't help blaming those men who brought slaves to this country for all this mess. Somehow, they are the ones that put my Mama and Daddy here, I just know it. I've also heard the

preacher say, "May God forgive them for their sins." I don't.
At least, not today.

ABOUT THE AUTHOR

Beverly Fisher graduated from the University of Memphis and Vanderbilt Law School. She has appeared on "60 Minutes" in an expose about insurance scams. She was a staff attorney for Legal Aid Society of Middle Tennessee for many years before going into private practice, focusing on Social Security Disability cases. She has climbed Mt. St. Helens and many Mayan pyramids, canoed countless Southern waterways, and hiked a multitude of trails. She lives in Tennessee surrounded by woods, wildlife, creeks, springs, dogs, and love.